Listen carefully to those who are silent.
~ Sana

*May you always dwell in the possibility
of a better tomorrow.*
~ Marjorie

MONSTRESS

VOLUME SIX
THE VOW

Collecting
MONSTRESS: TALK-STORIES Issues 1–2
& MONSTRESS Issues 31–35

MARJORIE LIU
WRITER

SANA TAKEDA
ARTIST

RUS WOOTON
LETTERING & DESIGN

JENNIFER M. SMITH
EDITOR

ERIKA SCHNATZ
PRODUCTION ARTIST

CERI RILEY
EDITORIAL ASSISTANT

MONSTRESS
created by
MARJORIE LIU &
SANA TAKEDA

TALK-STORIES: PART ONE

RAVENNA. PRESENT DAY.

"THE FEDERATION ARMY IS SENDING OUT RAIDING PARTIES TO SURROUNDING TOWNS.

"THEY DON'T CARE HOW MANY THEY KILL...THE CUMAEA DON'T NEED LIVING BODIES TO HARVEST LILIUM."

AND STILL THE COURTS DON'T SEND SUPPORT, EVEN WITH THE WARLORD HERE.

BAH. THE WARLORD IS MORE OBSESSED WITH HER WIFE'S BETRAYAL THAN TRYING TO STRATEGIZE AN OFFENSIVE.

HER WIFE... BEING THE BARONESS?

I'VE HEARD SO MUCH ABOUT THIS WOMAN, I FEEL AS IF I KNOW HER.

SOME WINE, LADY HALFWOLF?

NO. I USED TO DRINK TOO MUCH.
THAT'S ONE OLD PROBLEM I DEFINITELY DON'T NEED.

ER...YOU SHOULD AVOID THE EASTERN QUARTER. THE WARLORD IS SURVEYING FIRE DAMAGE.
DON'T LOSE YOUR FEATHERS, CORVIN. SHE WOULDN'T EVEN RECOGNIZE ME.

WE DIDN'T MAKE ENOUGH LAST NIGHT TO FEED THE STRAGGLERS. I DON'T WANT THAT HAPPENING AGAIN.
NO BELLY WILL BE FULL, BUT THERE'LL BE A BITE FOR EVERYONE.
WHAT ARE WE SUPPOSED TO DO WITH THAT STRANGE FOX CHILD?
LORD CORVIN SAID TO KEEP OUT OF HER WAY. SPOILED, IF YOU ASK ME. ALL THESE MOUTHS TO FEED, AND SHE COULD BE WASTING FOOD OVER THERE --
MISS!
YOU SHOULD BE RESTING. SOON ENOUGH, THERE WON'T BE MUCH TIME FOR SLEEP.
I LIKE BEING USEFUL.
MAKES ME FEEL BETTER. TAKES MY MIND OFF... EVERYTHING ELSE.
WHAT ARE YOU MAKING?
OH, I USED TO HANG AROUND THE KITCHENS AT THE REFUGEE CAMP. ALL THE LITTLE ONES DID BECAUSE WE WERE HUNGRY.
I WATCHED THE COOKS...AND THEN I'D MAKE BELIEVE WITH PRETEND INGREDIENTS.
BUT ONE TIME... I HELPED MAKE SOMETHING FOR REAL.

EVEN AFTER ALL THESE YEARS, THE BEST THING I EVER ATE WAS AT THE CAMP, WHEN MY FAMILY WAS ALIVE.
WHAT'S THE BEST THING YOU EVER ATE, MISS?
OH.
WELL, I'LL TELL YOU MINE.

COME ON, PERRI!
MOMMA IS GONNA LOVE WHAT WE SCAVENGED!
YOU THINK SO?
OF COURSE! SHE'S GOING TO MAKE SO MANY WONDERFUL THINGS! AND THEN WE CAN TRADE THEM FOR FOOD!
OR MAYBE AN EXTRA BLANKET? MY TAIL IS COLD AT NIGHT.
YOU'RE A MIRACLE WORKER, YOU REALLY ARE. I DIDN'T THINK ANYONE COULD FIX THAT OLD RADIO.
WELL, WE'LL SEE IF IT LASTS THE NIGHT.
MOMMA!
LOOK!
KSS

GODDESS, HOW DID YOU MANAGE TO FIND --
PERRI SCAVENGED ALL OF THIS FOR YOU! ISN'T THAT AMAZING?
BUT IT WAS BOTH OF --
IT'S JUNK.
I CAN'T DO ANYTHING WITH IT.
YOU HAVEN'T EVEN LOOKED...
SHE'LL ALWAYS HATE ME.
SHE DOESN'T HATE YOU.
DON'T LIE...YOU KNOW SHE DOES.
I'M NOT HERS.
SHE DIDN'T EVEN KNOW ABOUT ME UNTIL A COUPLE MONTHS AGO. JUST LIKE I DIDN'T KNOW ABOUT ANY OF *YOU.*
WE'RE SISTERS... THAT'S ALL THAT MATTERS.

IS THERE SOMETHING YOU WANT TO TELL ME?

THE GIRLS CAME HOME UPSET.
KIPPA EXPLAINED WHAT HAPPENED.
KIPPA SHOULD BE MORE LOYAL TO HER MOTHER.

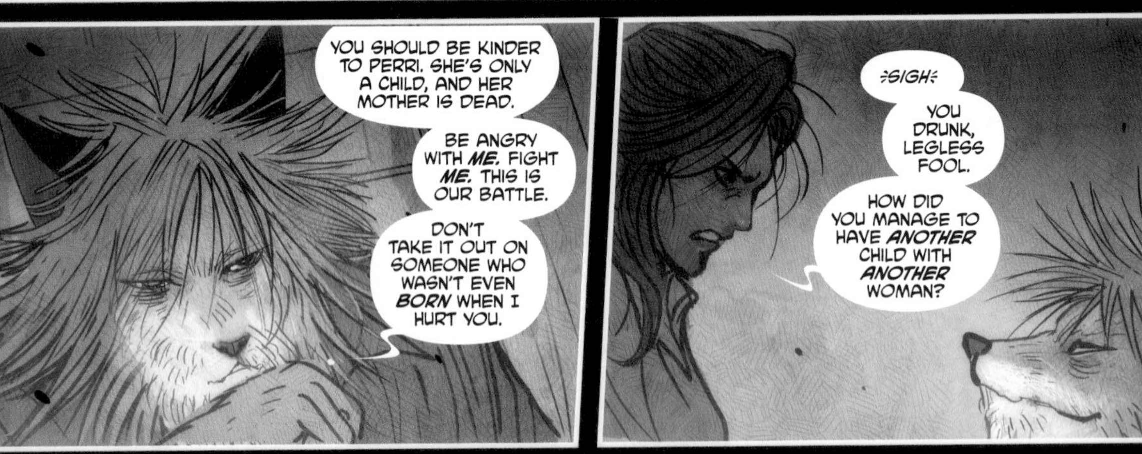
YOU SHOULD BE KINDER TO PERRI. SHE'S ONLY A CHILD, AND HER MOTHER IS DEAD.
BE ANGRY WITH *ME.* FIGHT *ME.* THIS IS OUR BATTLE.
DON'T TAKE IT OUT ON SOMEONE WHO WASN'T EVEN *BORN* WHEN I HURT YOU.
SIGH
YOU DRUNK, LEGLESS FOOL.
HOW DID YOU MANAGE TO HAVE *ANOTHER* CHILD WITH *ANOTHER* WOMAN?

SHE DIDN'T MIND THE STUMPS.
DON'T WORRY.
WE'RE GOING TO FIX IT.

WE'VE RUN OUT OF HARD SHELTERS, SO YOU'LL HAVE TO MAKE DO WITH A TENT UNTIL WE HAVE THE FUNDS TO PURCHASE MORE BOARD FOR WALLS.
FUCK SHELTER. WE HEARD THERE'S FOOD HERE. MY FAMILY HASN'T EATEN IN DAYS.
MEALS ARE DISPENSED AT STAGGERED TIMES THROUGHOUT THE DAY. YOU'LL BE GIVEN A SCHEDULE --
KIPPA, IF WE GET CAUGHT THE GUARDS'LL CUT OFF OUR TAILS.
THEY SAY THAT TO ACT BIG, BUT ONLY WITCHES CUT OFF TAILS.
WE'LL JUST GET YELLED AT...OR MAYBE KICKED.
KIPPA, IF YOU'VE COME WITH ANOTHER EXCUSE FROM YOUR FATHER --
NO, MRS. RIVESLEEK! POPPA FINISHED MENDING YOUR BRASSIERE. HE EVEN FOUND A REPLACEMENT WIRE!
HMPH. WELL, THEN. I GET PAID NEXT WEEK. I'LL BRING HIM HIS DUE THEN.
*MMM...*IN THE MEANTIME...I DON'T SUPPOSE YOU COULD DO ME AND MY SISTER A FAVOR?
DON'T TELL ANYONE I LET YOU IN. AND IF THE COOKS CATCH YOU --
WE SNUCK IN!
WOW, LOOK AT ALL THIS *FOOD.*

HURRY. FIND ANY VEGETABLE SCRAPS THAT LOOK FRESH.

WE CAN DIVIDE UP THIS LEFTOVER RICE AT THE END OF THE SHIFT! IT'LL BE A GOOD MEAL FOR US TONIGHT!

SIGH I HATE CUTTING DAIKON, AND OUR KNIVES ARE ALL DULL.
LILAH, WHERE'S THE WHETSTONE?!

I HAVEN'T HAD MEAT SINCE THE MOON FESTIVAL. AND IT WAS MOSTLY JUST MEAT *FLAVOR.*
THIS IS GOING TO WORK, PERRI. I PROMISE.

ZZZZZZZZ

WE'LL SAVE SOME OF THIS FOR ANOTHER MEAL.
WHAT DO I DO?
THE COOKS ALWAYS PEEL THE DAIKON BEFORE THEY USE IT. START THERE.
JUST CUT REALLY CLOSE TO THE SURFACE, SO YOU WASTE AS LITTLE AS POSSIBLE.
CHOP IT INTO CHUNKS.
DAIKON IS THICK, KIPPA! THE KNIFE DOESN'T WANT TO GO THROUGH!
LEAN IN!
SHHH... DON'T DROP IT. WE NEED TO BOIL THIS WATER.
WHAT ELSE GOES IN?
MMM...

EGG WHITES!
NOT THE YOLK?
WE SAVE THAT FOR ANOTHER DISH!
I THINK THAT'S THE MOST BEAUTIFUL THING I'VE EVER SEEN.
IT SMELLS GOOD ALREADY, DOESN'T IT? I'M NOT IMAGINING THAT?
I LOVE COOKING! IT'S ALMOST AS MUCH FUN AS EATING!
WHAT'S NEXT?!
FRIED RICE!

SIGH MEAT LOOKS GOOD!
WE DON'T HAVE ANY OIL, BUT THE SAUSAGE LOOKS FATTY.
IT SMELLS LIKE SO MUCH FAT!
I'VE NEVER HEARD SAUSAGE CRACKLE!
IT'S JUMPING!
SSZZZLLL
NOW WE ADD THAT EGG YOLK...
...AND THE RICE...
THIS IS HOW I'VE SEEN THE COOKS FRY RICE! THEY REALLY PUT A LOT OF FORCE INTO IT!
OH, KIPPA! IT SMELLS DELICIOUS.

GODDESS! WHAT ARE YOU DOING?!
WHERE IN THE WORLD DID YOU FIND --
OH, NO.
NO, NO, NO.
THE OTHERS WILL SMELL THIS, IF THEY HAVEN'T ALREADY. I COULD SMELL IT, DAMN IT.
THERE WILL BE SO MUCH TROUBLE IF IT'S FOUND OUT WE HAVE SPECIAL FOOD IN THE HOUSE. WE COULD BE KICKED OUT OF THE CAMP!
QUICK, EAT UP.
NO! THIS WAS FOR *YOU!* IT WAS SUPPOSED TO BE A GOOD SURPRISE!
SO YOU WOULD LOVE ME!
...YOU LITTLE FOOLS...

KIPPA, THE TRAP DOOR.

WAS SOMEONE COOKING... MEAT...IN HERE?
I WISH. I SMELLED THE SAME THING.
YOU KNOW HOW IT IS, THOUGH...SCENTS CARRY FROM THE CAMP KITCHEN.
DON'T YOU DARE BE ANGRY AT US.
NO... THIS IS MY FAULT.
I'M SORRY.
YOU CAN'T BUY LOVE, LITTLE ONES.
YOU COULD BEND YOURSELF BACKWARD INTO A KNOT, DO SOMERSAULTS TO THE MOON...
...BUT FOR SOME PEOPLE, THAT WOULD NEVER BE REASON ENOUGH TO LOVE YOU.
I *NEED* YOU TO LOVE ME.
NO, YOU DON'T.
KIPPA LOVES YOU. YOUR FATHER LOVES YOU.
IF YOU LOVE YOURSELF, THAT WILL BE ENOUGH.

DO YOU LOVE YOURSELF, MOMMA?
MOMMA?
WHEN YOUR FATHER WAKES UP AND THE CAMP HAS GONE TO BED, WE'LL EAT.

YOU SLY LITTLE FOXES. THAT IS THE MOST RIDICULOUS STORY I'VE EVER HEARD.
AND THE MOST DELICIOUS MEAL I'VE EVER HAD.
IT'S VERY GOOD.

YOU'VE NEVER TOLD ME ABOUT HER BEFORE.
YOUR SISTER.
I THINK I'VE CUT ENOUGH TO FEED A LOT OF PEOPLE.
WILL YOU HELP ME MAKE DAIKON SOUP?

TALK-STORIES: PART TWO

SNIFF
SNIFF
WIMPER
SNIFF
I BROKE MY WORD, MISS.
ALL THOSE CHILDREN DIED BECAUSE OF ME. ALL THE PEOPLE THE WITCHES KILLED...THAT'S MY FAULT, TOO.
I SHOULD DIE.
I SUPPOSE...
...IF YOU'RE A COWARD.

YOU CAN'T RUN FROM THOSE MISTAKES...YOU HAVE TO LIVE WITH THEM AND FIGURE OUT HOW TO MAKE THEM RIGHT.
BUT I DON'T THINK I CAN LIVE WITH THE PAIN, MISS. I CAN'T.
I WISH THE WITCHES HAD KILLED ME BACK IN ZAMORA.
YOU... WHO KEEPS FORGIVING ME AGAIN AND AGAIN FOR BEING A... MONSTER.
YOU...WHO ALWAYS FORGIVES MY CRUELTY, AND ANGER...
...YOU CAN'T FORGIVE YOURSELF?
THAT'S DIFFERENT, MISS.
WHY?
HMMM.
COME ON, I NEED YOUR HELP WITH SOMETHING.
EEP!

MY MOTHER ALWAYS SAID THAT HAPPY MEMORIES ARE A DOUBLE-EDGED SWORD.

YOU'LL CUT YOURSELF IF YOU LEAN ON THEM TOO MUCH.

SEIZI DISAGREED.

HE THOUGHT THE MORE HAPPINESS I HAD IN MY LIFE...THE STRONGER I WOULD BE.

THAT IT WOULD PROTECT ME.

AREKA!
NO ONE FOLLOWED YOU, DID THEY?
NO ONE CARES ENOUGH TO FOLLOW ME. I'M NOT THE THRONE-HEIR, REMEMBER? I DON'T EVEN HAVE FINS.
DO YOU THINK THIS WILL WORK?
I HEARD SEIZI SAYING NO ONE GOES TO THAT ISLAND BECAUSE IT'S TOO DANGEROUS.
NO ONE WILL EXPECT THAT WE'VE RUN AWAY THERE.
I HOPE NOT. I DON'T WANT TO BE SENT TO THE FEDERATION, MAIKA.
A MILITARY SCHOOL? IT'S HORRIBLE.

YOU'RE SURE ABOUT THE BOAT?
SEIZI HAD IT MADE FOR ME. I'M NOT SUPPOSED TO KNOW ABOUT IT YET, THOUGH.
GASP IT'S BEAUTIFUL.
AND SO SMALL.
IT'S PERFECT.
SEIZI HIRED BUILDERS WHO MAKE VESSELS FOR CATS, SO EVERYTHING SHOULD BE THE RIGHT SIZE FOR US.
MAIKA... EVERYONE IN THE CITY IS EITHER TERRIFIED OF THE IMURAS OR DEATH-LOYAL TO THEM.
BUT THEY'RE NOT *THAT* SCARY...ARE THEY?
MMM...I GUESS THAT DEPENDS.
JUST DON'T BE AN ENEMY...AND YOU *MIGHT* SURVIVE.
ER... OKAY.

NNGH!! THIS SAIL!
IT'S TOO HEAVY!
I'M COMING!
I WISH I WAS AS STRONG AS YOU. MAYBE THEN THE OTHERS WOULD OVERLOOK MY LEGS.
IT'S NOT YOUR FAULT YOU WERE BORN THAT WAY.
BOTH MY MOTHERS ARE SIRENS. IF ONE OF THEM WAS HUMAN, IT WOULD BE ALL RIGHT...BUT I'M A FREAK. I CAN'T EVEN SWIM WELL.
THE POETS SAY THAT HUMANS CAME FROM THE SEA. MAYBE YOU'RE PROOF OF THAT.
ONE OF MY ANCESTORS PROBABLY HAD HUMAN BLOOD AND NEVER TOLD ANYONE.
I'M PART HUMAN, TOO.
AND YOU CAN DO THINGS THEY CAN'T. YOU CAN GO PLACES THEY CAN'T.
THAT'S WHY THEY WANT TO SEND YOU AWAY. BECAUSE YOU'RE THE ONLY ONE OF THEM WHO CAN STUDY AT THAT SCHOOL.

SHARP KNIFE, FRESH FISH, GOOD LIFE.
THERE'S A STORM COMING.
WE NEED TO LOWER THE SAIL AND TIE EVERYTHING DOWN.

MAIKA, ARE WE OKAY?!
KRAKOOM
WE'RE GREAT!
LIGHTNING SQUIDS! I DIDN'T THINK THEY WERE REAL!
BECAUSE NO ONE SURVIVES THE EXPERIENCE!
FWHOP

AIEEEEEEE!!
HHHHUHHH!

WE'RE...
...OKAY...
AS IF THESE TWO THOUGHT THEY COULD HIDE FROM THE EYES OF THE SEA.
SILLY THINGS.
THEY'RE LUCKY TO BE ALIVE, COMMANDER.
WE SHOULD HAVE FETCHED THEM BEFORE THE STORM HIT. SEIZI WOULD HAVE BEEN MIGHTY SOUR IF THE HALFWOLF CHILD HAD DROWNED.
GOOD.

MY SON HAS ALWAYS BEEN TOO SOFT, OLD TOOTH.
ONE MUST GIVE THE WAVE EMPRESS A CHANCE TO EAT... EVEN IF WHAT SHE EATS IS OUR HEARTS.
IN MY OPINION, SHE GETS PLENTY ENOUGH TO EAT AS IT IS.

SSSIP
AH, THE FLOTSAM AWAKENS.
WHO ARE YOU? AND WHERE ARE WE?
CALM DOWN, WHELP.
NO, I WON'T! ANSWER ME!
REALLY? YOU DARE?

I'D FORGOTTEN WHAT "NO" EVEN SOUNDS LIKE.
AUGH!
AH. YOU DON'T GIVE UP, IS THAT IT?
OR ARE YOU JUST STUPID?
NNF!
KRAK
RAHH!
NO...
...IT'S SOMETHING DEEPER.
YARRGH!

I SUPPOSE I MIGHT UNDERSTAND WHY MY SON DOTES ON YOU, SOFT-HEART THAT HE IS.
YOU *DO* HAVE POTENTIAL... DESPITE BEING A WOLF.
SON?
ARE YOU... SEIZI AND KENZI'S MOTHER?
INDEED, I DID GIVE BIRTH TO THOSE MISCREANTS.
NOW COME WITH ME. MIGHT AS WELL ROUSE YOUR FRIEND, TOO.
MAIKA... THAT'S SAURI IMURA. A HUNDRED YEARS AGO SHE WAS THE FIRST OF THE BLOOD QUEENS TO RULE THYRIA AS CONSORT TO THE SIREN QUEEN, BUT THEN --
-- THEN I DECIDED I'D MUCH RATHER BE A SAVAGE CONQUERER THAN A BORED QUEEN.
NOW, STOP WITH THE LIPS.
WE CAN'T STAY HERE. WE WERE ON OUR WAY --
-- TO THE ISLAND YOU NOTED IN MY SON'S MAP BOOK?
PAH. YOU HAVE ARRIVED, WOLF CHILD.

YOU'RE MAKING THAT UP! SEIZI SAID IT'S A DANGEROUS PLACE!
AM I NOT DANGEROUS?
HOW WOULD I KNOW? ALL YOU DID WAS WIN A FIGHT AGAINST A CHILD.
MAIKA! HUSH!
OH, YOU ARE A SPITTY ONE.
I LIKE THAT.
COMMANDER, A SEABIRD ARRIVED. SEIZI AND LADY HALFWOLF WILL BE ARRIVING BY SUNDOWN TOMORROW.
SEND A REPLY.
TELL MY SON...THAT I SENT THE CHILDREN TO MY SISTER...HMMM... IN AJABARA.
COMMANDER... THAT'S A WEEK'S SAIL FROM HERE.
YES... AND ANOTHER WEEK'S JOURNEY BACK.
HE NEEDS TO SEE HIS AUNT, ANYWAY.
CHILDREN, WELCOME TO THE OUTERMOST RING OF THE SPICE ISLANDS.
A MONTH OF HARD SAILING WOULD BARELY ALLOW YOU TO SEE THE VAST HOLDINGS THAT I, MY SISTERS, AND MY DAUGHTERS CONTROL.
AND FOR THE NEXT TWO WEEKS, YOU HAVE THE RUN OF IT.

"LITTLE FOX...I WISH I COULD SAY THE LAST CAREFREE WEEKS OF MY EARLY LIFE WERE SPENT WITH MY MOTHER...
"...BUT IT WAS THAT PIRATE QUEEN WHO ALLOWED ME TO BE A CHILD...BRIEFLY.
"I HAVEN'T THOUGHT ABOUT HER IN YEARS...NOT EVEN WHEN YOU AND I WERE IN THYRIA.
"I FORGOT IT ALL. I PUT IT AWAY."
"DO YOU WISH YOU WERE THERE NOW, MISS?
"MISS?"

THE ANCIENTS WHO ALLIED THEMSELVES WITH THE WAVE EMPRESS AND HER DAUGHTERS BUILT A KINGDOM AWAY FROM THEIR OWN KIND.
MY MOTHER IS ONE OF THOSE ANCIENTS -- THE TIGER QUEEN.
SHE BUILT THIS TEMPLE TO HELP HER REMEMBER.
REMEMBER WHAT?
THE HOME SHE LEFT BEHIND, SHE SAID. BUT SHE WOULD NEVER TELL ME OR MY SISTERS WHERE THAT WAS.
SHE SAID I WOULDN'T UNDERSTAND.
I'M TOLD THAT EVEN THE SHAMAN-EMPRESS CAME HERE TO STUDY THIS PLACE.
DON'T TELL MY MOTHER THAT. SHE'S OBSESSED WITH HER.

ZZZZZZZ
I DON'T WANT TO LEAVE THIS PLACE. *EVER.*
HMM.
SO YOU'RE BOTH BEING SENT TO THE FEDERATION TO LEARN HUMAN WAR TACTICS?
QUAINT.
YOUR MOTHER SHOULD HAVE SENT YOU TO ME.
YOU'RE A GREAT WARRIOR?
HA! I'M A SIMPLE TIGER WHO ONLY KNOWS TWO THINGS.
HOW TO SURVIVE... AND HOW TO THRIVE.
MY MOTHER THINKS I HAVE TO BE THE BEST FIGHTER, THE BEST AT WARCRAFT, OR I'LL DIE.
SHE SHOULD HAVE JUST SENT YOU SAILING.
THERE IS NO MORE SAVAGE TEACHER THAN THE SEA, CHILD.
REMEMBER THAT, WHEN THE DANGER COMES. FIGHT LIKE THE SEA. THE SEA IS RELENTLESS. IT NEVER STOPS. IT HAS NO PITY. IT DEVOURS.
WHAT IF I DON'T WANT TO DEVOUR ANYONE? WHAT IF I HATE FIGHTING AND KILLING?

I AM A QUEEN OF THE SEA, NOT BECAUSE I AM FEARLESS...AND NOT BECAUSE I LOVE VIOLENCE OR HOLDING POWER OVER THOSE WEAKER THAN ME.
THEN HOW?
HMMM.
WHY DID YOU RUN AWAY?
BECAUSE I DON'T WANT TO GO TO MILITARY SCHOOL IN THE FEDERATION.
I'M AFRAID.
AFRAID? I DON'T THINK SO.
IF YOU WERE REALLY AFRAID YOU WOULD HAVE STAYED HOME AND FOLLOWED YOUR MOTHER'S WISHES.
INSTEAD, YOU SAILED INTO THE UNKNOWN.
BUT THAT'S LESS SCARY!
OH, CHILD.
HOW I SYMPATHIZE. I REMEMBER MY OWN EDUCATION.
GO TO THE FEDERATION. LEARN ALL YOU CAN, AND DON'T FORGET THAT YOU TRIED TO FIGHT AGAINST YOUR FATE. THAT'S IMPORTANT.
JUST DON'T MAKE A HABIT OUT OF RUNNING AWAY.
AND IF WE EVER MEET AGAIN...
...YOU MAY CALL ME AUNTIE.

MISS, YOU HAD SUCH A GOOD LIFE... WITH FRIENDS AND PEOPLE WHO LOVED YOU.
MISS?

CHAPTER THIRTY-ONE

Tuya...
...There are days I would give anything to see you again...
...And there are days I hope that I never do.
You might hate me now, for what I have embraced.
You might hate me for choosing to live instead of die.
THE SAME KILLER IS TARGETING OUR PATROLS AND RAIDING PARTIES, COLONEL ANUWAT.
KILLERS, YOU MEAN.
NO. THE SURVIVORS INSIST IT'S ONLY A YOUNG WOMAN AND SOME...DEMONIC APPARITION.
Which would be fitting, because I hate myself for that choice, too.
And yet, I can't help it, Tuya.
SHE FITS THE DESCRIPTION OF THE... UM, HUMAN... YOU WERE INTERROGATING.
WELL.
WE ALL KNOW A HUMAN DIDN'T DO THIS.
Part of me still has hope.
ISN'T THAT RIGHT, OFFICER?
Y-YES, COLONEL.

DAUGHTER... HOW GOOD IT IS TO SEE YOU EATING. I FIND MYSELF...DELIGHTED... THAT YOU HAVE BEGUN TO TAKE RESPONSIBILITY FOR YOUR HUNGER.
MINDFULNESS *IS* BETTER, IS IT NOT? BETTER THAN FEARING WHO YOU MIGHT HARM SHOULD YOUR HUNGER RAGE OUT OF CONTROL?
NO, IT'S ***NOT*** BETTER. KILLING OTHERS TO SURVIVE IS A FUCKING NIGHTMARE.
BUT DAUGHTER... NOW YOU ACCEPT IT AS PART OF YOUR NATURE...AND *THAT* IS A START.
A START TO WHAT, OLD MAN?
WHERE DOES THE HUNGER END? DOES IT JUST BECOME SOMETHING ELSE THAT'S EVEN MORE AWFUL?

DAUGHTER... IT IS NOT THE HUNGER THAT TRANSFORMS.
HUNGER IS THE FUEL. BUT IT IS YOU...YOU... WHO BECOMES SOMETHING ELSE.
WHETHER YOU BECOME ABERRANT OR GLORIOUS... THAT IS UP TO YOU.
MY MOTHER GAVE ME SIMILAR ADVICE. IT WAS SHITTY THEN, AND IT'S SHITTY NOW.
WHY ARE YOU IN MY DREAMS, OLD MAN?
I KNOW THIS IS REAL. SOMEHOW YOU WIGGLED YOUR WAY INTO MY HEAD.
YES, EASILY. A GOD SLIPPED FROM MY BLOOD TO YOURS. THERE IS NO CLOSER BOND.
I AM HERE TO REMIND US *BOTH* OF THAT CONNECTION. OF ITS VITAL IMPORTANCE...TO OUR FUTURES.
WE NEED EACH OTHER, DAUGHTER. THOUGH I AM, PERHAPS, MORE COMFORTABLE WITH THAT IDEA THAN YOU ARE.
UH-HUH. SO WHAT'S ABOUT TO HAPPEN?
WHAT HAVE YOU DONE NOW?
OLD MAN?
REALLY? FUCK YOU.

SIGH
WHAT DID YOU MAKE OF THAT?
...HE WANTED... YOU TO KNOW...YOU ARE NOT SAFE... IN YOUR OWN MIND...THAT YOU ARE HIS...ANY TIME HE WISHES...

...HE HAD NO INFORMATION...TO GIVE...EXCEPT THAT...
CLEARLY. BUT THAT WASN'T ALL OF IT.

...CHILD... THE FIRST CHANCE...
...KILL HIM... DO NOT HESITATE...
...HE UNDID ME...REACHED INTO ME...AND I AM STILL... WOUNDED...
ZINN...
...ABOUT WHAT I SAW INSIDE YOUR MEMORIES. THE CHILD, AND THE HUMAN, MARIUM --

...NO...
STOP. IT MATTERS, ZINN. I NEED TO KNOW WHY THE ANCIENTS WERE TRYING TO KILL THE CHILD.
...FOR THE SAME REASON...THEY WILL TRY TO KILL...YOU...
...FOR YOUR POWER...FOR WHAT...YOU CAN...UNDO...

ZINN! FUCK!
ER, MISS?

I'M SO GLAD YOU FINALLY WOKE UP. LORD CORVIN SENT ME TO FIND YOU.
THE WARLORD'S AIR FLEET IS COMING.
IT'LL BE HERE BY EVENING.

PONTUS.
"WELL, IS IT ANY SURPRISE THAT WE RAN OUT OF TIME? IT DOESN'T MATTER WHETHER RAVENNA STANDS OR FALLS, THE DAMAGE IS DONE. THE FEDERATION AND THE ARCANIC COURTS ARE NOW AT WAR."
BUT, GIVEN THE INFORMATION YOU'VE JUST SHARED, ADMIRAL BRITO, PERHAPS WE CAN HOPE FOR A QUICK RESOLUTION.
CAN WE? IT IS A SHOCKING REQUEST.
I MYSELF AM SURPRISED AT THE AUDACITY OF THE DUSK COURT'S DEMAND.
EXTERMINATE ALL THE CUMAEA?
IT'S BRILLIANT.
THE CUMAEA HAVE THE FEDERATION UNDER THEIR THUMBS. THEY'RE THE REASON THIS WAR IS HAPPENING.
REMOVE THEM FROM POWER AND ORDER IS RESTORED.
YOU DON'T SIMPLY STAMP OUT A RELIGION.
NOR DO YOU MURDER THOUSANDS SIMPLY BECAUSE OF THAT RELIGION.

WE MAY NOT AGREE WITH THE PATH THE CUMAEA HAVE LED US DOWN, BUT ALMOST ALL OF US HAVE FAMILY WHO ARE PART OF THEIR ORDER.
THE ADMIRAL IS RIGHT. THIS IS AN IMPOSSIBLE REQUEST.
AND LET US SAY YOU AGREE. LET US IMAGINE YOU CARRY THROUGH AND MURDER THEM ALL.
THE FEDERATION WOULD TURN ON ITSELF OVER THAT CHOICE -- HUMANS AGAINST HUMANS.

OR THEY WOULD BLAME US.

IF I MIGHT INTERRUPT A MOMENT -- I HAVE ANOTHER PROPOSITION, FOR YOUR CONSIDERATION.

AS YOU KNOW, THE WAVE COURT HAS BEEN GRANTED PERMISSION FROM THE WAVE EMPRESS HERSELF TO DECIDE WHETHER OR NOT TO PARTICIPATE IN THIS SECOND CONFLICT.
JUST PRIOR TO THIS MEETING, I WAS INFORMED THAT THE WAVE COURT HAS MADE AT LEAST *ONE* DECISION.

OUR ANCIENTS WILL GRANT THE FEDERATION NAVY PROTECTION FROM THE SEA. BUT ONLY IF IT ABSTAINS FROM THE WAR, OR ALLIES ITSELF WITH THE ARCANIC COURTS.
SHOULD YOU FIGHT FOR THE FEDERATION...
...YOU WILL SUFFER ABSOLUTE DESTRUCTION.

HOLY CITY OF AURUM, CAPITAL OF THE FEDERATION.
WE'RE CURSED!
IT'S A LIE THEY CAN'T SEE US! LOOK! THEIR EYES ARE WATCHING!
CITIZENS! DO NOT BE AFRAID! MARIUM IS WITH YOU! THESE ARE ILLUSIONS CAST BY THE DEMONS --
SHUT UP! THIS IS YOUR FAULT!
FWAK
WE CAN'T LISTEN TO THE CUMAEA!
IT'S THE WAR! WE'RE BEING PUNISHED FOR KILLING ARCANICS!
SIGH REALLY? MUST OUR SISTER-BROTHERS BE SO OBVIOUS?
I SUPPOSE THE PRISON WALLS ARE THINNING IF THEY CAN SENSE THE MASK.
SUCH POWERS OF OBSERVATION YOU POSSESS.

YOU, FINISH YOUR REPORT. HOW GOES OUR LILIUM HARVESTS?

AS A-ALWAYS, THE S-SCIENTISTS ARE DOING THEIR B-BEST TO MAXIMIZE LILIUM LOADS, BUT WE NEED MORE B-BODIES.

F-FORTUNATELY, COLONEL ANUWAT'S R-RAIDS AROUND RAVENNA HAVE BEEN P-PROVIDING US WITH NEW STOCK.

SPEAKING OF ANUWAT...WE SENT HER OUR BLESSED LITTLE ONES.

HOW HAVE THEIR PHYSICAL ENHANCEMENTS HELD UP UNDER THE REALITIES OF BATTLE?

NOT WELL. ONLY TWO SURVIVED, WITH INJURIES -- THE S-SISTERS ODILE AND ZORTIA.

WE DON'T KNOW HOW THE OTHERS D-DIED, AS THEIR HANDLER PERISHED IN RAVENNA...

...AND THE INQUISITRIXES HAMMER AND NEEDLE HAVE GONE SILENT.

WHAT AN *EXPENSIVE* DISAPPOINTMENT.

SEND ORDERS FOR SISTERS ODILE AND ZORTIA TO BE EXTERMINATED SO WE CAN RECYCLE THE LILIUM IN THEIR BODIES.

I DON'T WANT TO WASTE A PRECIOUS RESOURCE ON ANYTHING DEFECTIVE.

YES, HOLY MOTHER!

HAMMER AND NEEDLE ARE AN UNACCEPTABLE LOOSE END, GULL.

THEY SAW YOUR TRUE FORM. YOU SHOULD HAVE KILLED THEM.

I WAS RATHER PREOCCUPIED WITH BEING POSSESSED, AND THEN EXPERIMENTED ON.

YES...***THAT.*** YOU ***HAVE*** VASTLY CHANGED SINCE WE LAST SAW EACH OTHER.

WHERE IS YOUR FIGHT? YOUR WIT? YOUR FOCUS?

YOU SOUND... ALMOST MORTAL.

AMUSED, ARE YOU? DON'T BE.
SOMETHING IS WRONG. OLD DAGON AND DREAMER REFUSE TO SEE IT.
I WAS NOT DECEIVED. A DEFILED OVERPOWERED MY WILL THROUGH THE MASK, AND COMPELLED ME TO ACT FOR IT.
YOU CANNOT IMAGINE THE FILTH THAT STILL COATS ME.
YOU FORGET MY HISTORY WITH THE DEFILED. I MOST CERTAINLY CAN IMAGINE, GULL. I REMEMBER WHAT THEY DID TO ME WITH PERFECT, EXCRUCIATING CLARITY.
AND I AM SORRY.
...THANK YOU.
I FEAR FOR US IF THE FALLEN HOUSES HAVE LOST CONTROL. WE CAN'T OPEN THE PRISON UNTIL WE KNOW FOR CERTAIN.
I WON'T ALLOW IT.
YOU... WON'T ALLOW IT?
DON'T SAY THOSE WORDS, EVEN IN JEST.
DREAMER HEARS ALL.
AND THE DREAMER SAYS THE SONG IS PURE.
I MUST, AS SUCH, BELIEVE IT WAS JUST AN UNFORTUNATE COINCIDENCE THAT A DEFILED REACHED THROUGH THE MASK.
YOUR WISDOM IS APPRECIATED.
YOU'RE RIGHT. I WAS MISTAKEN. I WON'T BRING IT UP AGAIN.
EXCELLENT.

WELCOME, OH DIVINE OVERSEERS OF MARIUM'S WILL! WELCOME TO THE INNER SANCTUM OF THE SHAMAN-EMPRESS' LAB! WE ARE BLESSED AND HUMBLED THAT YOU WOULD GRACE US WITH YOUR --
OH, BE SILENT. HAVE YOU LEARNED YET WHAT IS POWERING THE SHIELD SURROUNDING THAT BOX?
ALAS, NO -- AND OUR ATTEMPTS TO PENETRATE IT HAVE BEEN MET WITH...MAXIMUM RESISTANCE.
NEVER FEAR, HOWEVER! SCIENCE SHALL PREVAIL, MOST HOLY OF HOLY MOTHERS.
WE SHOULD ASK MAIKA'S FATHER. I HAVE NO DOUBT HE KNOWS HOW TO LOWER THIS SHIELD.
ANOTHER EXPERT? I WOULD BE DELIGHTED TO CONFER --
BE QUIET, GULL.
I WANT MORE GUARDS DOWN HERE.

"IN FACT, I WANT THE ENTIRE GARRISON DEFENDING THIS ROOM.
"BUILD A FORTRESS AROUND IT, IF YOU HAVE TO."
WELCOME TO AURUM, LORD WOLFE.
WHAT BRINGS YOU TO OUR FAIR CITY?
OH, I'M LOOKING FOR A VERY SPECIAL GIFT...
...FOR MY *DAUGHTER.*

HER FEVER ISN'T GOING DOWN?
NO. IF WE WERE HOME IN THE NORTH, I'D CARRY BETTANI INTO THE MOUNTAINS AND PACK HER IN SNOW.
OR USE WILLOW-WORT. THERE SHOULD BE SOME GROWING OUTSIDE THE CITY --

ABSOLUTELY NOT.
DON'T YOU FUCKING DARE.

THE WARLORD PLANS ON USING HER AIRSHIPS TO DESTROY THE FEDERATION ARMY.
SHE'LL WASTE FIREPOWER AND FUEL. THE HUMANS ARE TOO HIDDEN. SHE'LL HAVE TO BOMB THE ENTIRE FOREST FROM HERE TO THE WALL.
BETTER TO EVACUATE, LACE THE CITY WITH MINES AND TRIPWIRES, AND LEAVE BEHIND AN ASSASSINS UNIT TO KEEP PICKING THEM OFF.

I'LL SUGGEST IT. BUT THE WARLORD HAS CLASSICAL VALUES WHEN IT COMES TO WAR.
YOU MEAN, SHE BELIEVES IN *RULES...*
...AND HER *PRIDE* IS LINKED TO THOSE RULES.

UNFORTUNATLY, YOU'RE NO LONGER IN A POSITION TO DO ANYTHING ABOUT IT.
WITH THE WARLORD HERE, YOU DO NOT HAVE POWER IN RAVENNA. THE KIND OF POWER YOU NEED, WHICH IS POLITICAL AND SUBTLE.
HOW DOES SOMEONE GET THAT POWER?

ALLIES. CONNECTIONS. EXCHANGES OF FAVORS.
OH, YOU ***HAVE*** ALLIES! MISTER SEIZI...CORVIN, ME, MASTER REN, MISS VIHN? EVEN THE LEADERS IN PONTUS, FOR HOW YOU SAVED THE CITY.
SHE NEEDS MORE THAN THAT, KIPPA.

WELL...WHAT'S WRONG WITH JUST ***TALKING*** TO THE WARLORD? AND MAKING HER AN ALLY?
YOU'VE NEVER EVEN MET, HAVE YOU?
YOU THINK SHE WANTS TO HURT MISS, BUT MAYBE IT'S BECAUSE SHE DOESN'T KNOW HER.

IT'S MORE COMPLICATED THAN THAT, KIPPA.

KIPPA, I NEED TO BORROW THE NECKLACE I GAVE YOU.
OH, OF COURSE... IT'S YOURS, MISS.
NO. I'LL GIVE IT BACK.

LADY HALFWOLF --
FOCUS ON YOUR SISTER, CROW.

WELL, MOTHER.
I SUPPOSE IT'S TIME.

...WHAT... ARE YOU DOING...?
NOT RUNNING. TAKING A CHANCE.
MY OLD WAYS AREN'T GOING TO WORK ANYMORE, ZINN. THERE'S TOO MUCH AT STAKE.

...CHILD...
...I CANNOT DENY...YOU HAVE SHOWN... GROWTH...
...BUT I... FEAR...YOUR INSTINCTS...

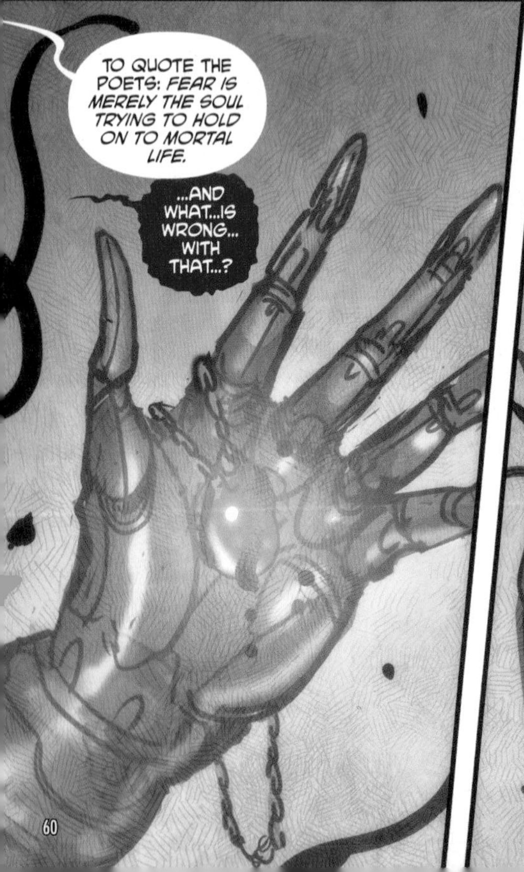
TO QUOTE THE POETS: *FEAR IS MERELY THE SOUL TRYING TO HOLD ON TO MORTAL LIFE.*
...AND WHAT...IS WRONG... WITH THAT...?

WE'RE NOT GOING TO SURVIVE IF WE DON'T RISK OUR LIVES, ZINN.
...THAT... IS THE LOGIC...OF IDIOTS...
WELL, WE'LL SEE WHAT THIS IDIOT CAN DO, WON'T WE?

KIPPA AND I ARE LEAVING, CROW.
YOU WERE RIGHT. THIS IS NO PLACE FOR US.
WHERE WILL YOU GO?
PONTUS. I NEED SEIZI'S NETWORK IF I'M GOING TO FIND THE REST OF THIS MASK.

I'LL MISS YOU. YOU'VE BEEN SUCH A GOOD FRIEND.
PLEASE STAY ALIVE. YOU AND YOUR SISTER.
OH.

MAY THE GODDESS PROTECT YOU, KIPPA.
YOU'RE CERTAIN OF THIS?
IT'S TIME. I CAN'T AVOID IT ANY LONGER.

THANK YOU FOR NOT LEAVING ME BEHIND, MISS.
I'M SURPRISED YOU SAID YES. THERE ARE STILL FOXES HERE.

I CAN'T BE AROUND THEM RIGHT NOW. NOT AFTER WHAT I DID...HOW I BROKE MY WORD.
BESIDES... I KNOW I CAN LEARN THINGS FROM YOU.
THAT'S A TERRIBLE IDEA.

THE BARONESS WILL KILL YOU FOR LETTING HER GO.
SHE SHOULD HAVE GIVEN *ME* THE POISON.
TANNO, TELL THE BARONESS THAT THE HALFWOLF HAS LEFT RAVENNA FOR GOOD.
I THINK YOU'LL FIND THAT THIS IS THE ONE TIME SHE'LL BE PLEASED BY YOUR BAD NEWS.
WE'LL KNOW SOON ENOUGH, CORVIN.
YOU SHOULD HAVE LEFT RAVENNA WITH THE HALFWOLF.

YOU'RE CERTAIN?
...ZZT...I SAW IT MYSELF...ZZT...THE HALFWOLF IS GONE...ZZT...
...ZZT... SHOULD I FOLLOW... ZZT...
BARONESS, THE WARLORD HAS COMMANDED YOUR PRESENCE IN RAVENNA...
I'M AFRAID I CAN'T AFFORD TO DISOBEY HER.
STAY, TANNO. I MIGHT NEED YOU.
HELLO, WIFE.

WOOOOOSH

TELL THE OTHER COMMANDERS THAT IF THEY EVER AGAIN OBEY MY WIFE -- *WITHOUT DIRECT ORDERS FROM ME* -- I'LL DO WORSE THAN THIS TO THEM.
YOU ARE SO WASTEFUL.
BOMB THE FOREST.
BURN THE HUMANS OUT.
IF YOU THINK THEY'RE STILL THERE, WAITING TO BE BOMBARDED --
CONFER WITH THE LOCALS AND ORGANIZE A SCOUTING PARTY. CONFIRM THE LOCATION OF THE HUMAN ARMY -- AND THEN STRIKE.
Y-YES, WARLORD.
YOU COMMITTED TREASON. I SHOULD KILL YOU.
WORSE, YOU FAILED.
I LEARNED SOMETHING IMPORTANT.
AND I LEARNED I CAN'T TRUST YOU.
YOU ALREADY KNEW THAT. AND YET, I'M NOT THE ONE WITH MY HEAD CUT IN HALF.

SABOTAGE? YOU'RE SURE?
OF COURSE. WE ONLY FINISHED REPAIRS A DAY AGO. MY OWN PEOPLE ARE GUARDING THE CANNONS NOW.
THEN THE FEDERATION HAS INFILTRATED OUR RANKS.

THAT WOULD BE PREFERABLE.
BUT THE SABOTEURS KILLEC THEMSELVES WITH POISON. IT TURNED THEIR GUMS WHITE, MADE THEIR BREAT SMELL LIKE... VANILLA.
ONLY ONE ROOT DOE THAT...AND GROWS IN T MOUNTAIN NORTH OF THE DUSK COURT.

NO, ENOUGH WITH YOUR CONSPIRACIES.
THE ANCIENTS WOULD NOT SABATOGE MY WEAPONS TO PROTECT A LILIUM REFINERY. THAT IS INSANITY.
WHY ARE YO SO BLIND?

BECAUSE I FIGHT REAL WARS, NOT PRETEND WARS.

AND YOU'VE ALMOST COST ME THIS WAR, WHEN WE'VE BARELY BEGUN.
ONE COULD ALMOST IMAGINE *YOU'RE* THE ONE WORKING FOR THE HUMANS.

YOU ARE SO TREACHEROUS.
YOU WEAR SO MANY MASKS, TELL SO MANY LIES AND HALF-TRUTHS. DO YOU EVEN KNOW WHO YOU ARE?
OR WHAT YOU REALLY WANT?
IT'S NOT ME, I KNOW THAT.

Hope is a strange feeling, Tuya.
Hope is frightening.
What is hope, except the possibility of disappointment?
And yet...I've learned that hope is just another kind of hunger.
Hope is another kind of fuel.
To hope...is to ask for a possibility, just a chance, at something better.
GASP
The smallest, most fragile hope will keep a person fighting, no matter how impossible the odds. I know this now.

And I hope, Tuya.
Oh, I hope.
I hope that if I stay alive long enough...I can become someone new.
That I can do some kind of good that will outweigh the bad.
That one day, I can be worthy of your love.
Of any kind of love.

Isn't that odd?
I never used to hope. That was your job. You had enough hope for the both of us.
You had hope for me.
Until you didn't.
I might not have remembered your eyes...but I remember that.

An excerpt from a lecture by the esteemed **Professor Tam Tam,** former First Record-Keeper of the Is'hami Temple, and learned contemporary of Namron Black Claw...
IT IS A LITTLE-KNOWN TRUTH THAT CATS ONCE WALKED FREELY BETWEEN WORLDS.
PERHAPS WE STILL DO, AND THOSE LUCKY ENOUGH TO CROSS OVER SIMPLY DO NOT SPEAK OF THEIR ADVENTURES. SUCH SECRECY WOULD NO DOUBT BE WISE. WE NO LONGER LIVE IN THE AGE OF ADARA FARCLAW, WHERE WORLDWALKING WAS AN EXPERIENCE OF JOY AND LEARNING, INSTEAD OF SOMETHING TO FEAR.
IT IS SAID THAT ADARA FARCLAW KEPT DETAILED ACCOUNTS OF HER ADVENTURES, BUT MOST OF THOSE HAVE BEEN LOST. WHAT HAS SURVIVED ARE FRAGMENTS OF HER PHILOSOPHIES, WHICH UNDERPINNED THE FOUNDATION OF THE EMPIRE SHE LATER ESTABLISHED.
THE MOST IMPORTANT OF THESE PHILOSOPHIES, IN HER WORDS?
"KINDNESS IS A POWER."
ACROSS EVERY WORLD, IN EVERY REALM SHE VISITED, ADARA FARCLAW OBSERVED HOW THE SMALLEST ACT OF KINDNESS, EVEN AGAINST MONUMENTAL CRUELTY, COULD CREATE A RIPPLE OF UNEXPECTED CONSEQUENCES THAT IN TIME MIGHT DEVASTATE THE MOST FEARSOME OF DOMINIONS.
"UBASTI TAKES GREAT JOY IN UNINTENDED CONSEQUENCES," ADARA WROTE, *"AND THERE IS NO MORE DIVINE REVERBERATION THAN THE ONE THAT COMES FROM GENTLE ACTS... TO OTHERS, AND TO ONE'S OWN SELF."*

THE POETS, WITHOUT ATTRIBUTION TO THE FARCLAW PHILOSOPHIES, HAVE LONG SAID THAT KINDNESS WRAPS TAIL WITH COMPASSION, THAT COMPASSION WRAPS TAIL WITH LOVE, AND THAT THIS TRINITY OF GRACE IS A REDOUBT AGAINST WHICH NO FORCE OF FEAR OR DARKNESS CAN PREVAIL.
ADARA FARCLAW PUT IT ANOTHER WAY:
"THE GENTLE HEART AND ITS ACTS ARE THE KEYS TO ENLIGHTENMENT, AND WILL OPEN DOORS TO WORLDS YOU HAVE NEVER IMAGINED."
HOLD THAT LESSON CLOSE, KITS.
AND ASK YOURSELVES THIS: WHEN ADARA FARCLAW SPOKE OF KEYS AND DOORS, WAS SHE SPEAKING ONLY OF PHILOSOPHIES...
...OR WAS SHE TEACHING US HOW TO TAKE OUR OWN FIRST STEPS UPON THE ROAD BETWEEN WORLDS?

CHAPTER THIRTY-TWO

GODDESS.
I BEG YOU. PLEASE WATCH OVER BETTANI. FILL HER WITH YOUR HEALING LIGHT. LET YOUR LOVE MOVE THROUGH HER.
GIVE HER THE STRENGTH TO LIVE AND FIGHT.
AND FORGIVE ME... IF YOU CAN.
FORGIVE ME FOR FOLLOWING THE TRUTH OF WHAT I KNOW IN MY HEART.
EVEN IF IT MEANS BRINGING SHAME UPON MY FAMILY.

PERHAPS WITH THE WARLORD'S AIRSHIPS WE CAN BEGIN A PROPER EVACUATION OF THE WOUNDED.
I WOULDN'T COUNT ON IT.
KIPPA?! WHAT ARE YOU DOING HERE?!
LORD CORVIN! I FOUND SOME WILLOW-WORT FOR YOUR SISTER'S FEVER, JUST OUTSIDE THE CITY!
BUT...YOU SHOULD BE FAR FROM HERE. VERY, *VERY* FAR.
OH, SORRY ABOUT THAT.
BUT I GUESS MISS ALWAYS INTENDED TO COME RIGHT BACK.
SHE SAID THE BARONESS HAS TOO MANY SPIES.
MISS WANTED HER TO THINK SHE'D LEFT RAVENNA.
GODDESS, NO.

MAIKA!
WIFE, MOVE AWAY!

YOU VILE DEGENERATE.
YOU DARE TRESSPASS INTO MY QUARTERS?
I'LL CUT YOUR EYES OUT.

DIDN'T YOU FUCKING HEAR ME?

...
WHERE DID YOU GET THAT NECKLACE?

AUNTIE.
I HEARD YOU'VE BEEN LOOKING FOR ME.

GUARDS, SEIZE HER.

REALLY, THIS IS HOW YOU TREAT YOUR ONLY NIECE?

NO WONDER YOU WEREN'T GRANDMOTHER'S FAVORITE. OR ANYONE ELSE'S.

YOU EVEN SOUND LIKE MORIKO. SHE WAS ALWAYS QUICK WITH THE CHEAP INSULT.

IT'S NOT CHEAP WHEN IT'S TRUE.

GAH!

YOU SHOULD REALLY LEARN TO CONTROL YOURSELF, AUNTIE.

A VIOLENT TEMPER IS SO UNATTRACTIVE.

WOULDN'T YOU AGREE... BARONESS?

WSSHHH

CALM DOWN.

YOUR SISTER IS DEAD. TAKING OUT YOUR ANGER ON HER DAUGHTER IS UNPRODUCTIVE, NO MATTER HOW *ANNOYING* SHE IS.

AND... IT'S FAR TOO PUBLIC FOR THIS CONVERSATION.

TAKE THE HALFWOLF TO THE WARLORD'S AIRSHIP. TELL THE NEW CAPTAIN TO STAND DOWN PREPARATIONS FOR BATTLE AND PREPARE INSTEAD FOR DEPARTURE.
YOU SEEM TO HAVE ALREADY FORGOTTEN THAT YOU DON'T GIVE ORDERS HERE, WIFE.
HEH. THAT'S NOT WHAT I'VE HEARD.
YOU. LAUGH ALL YOU LIKE...
...BUT YOU WILL TELL ME EVERYTHING YOU KNOW ABOUT THE WEAPON THAT DESTROYED CONSTANTINE. YOUR MOTHER'S WEAPON.
EVEN IF I HAVE TO TEAR HER SECRETS FROM YOU, SCREAM BY SCREAM.
MY MOTHER'S WEAPON?
I'M SURPRISED YOU HAVEN'T ASKED YOUR WIFE.
SHE KNOWS EXACTLY WHAT DESTROYED CONSTANTINE. SHE WAS THERE, AFTER ALL. WITH ME.
SHE KNOWS ALL MY SECRETS.

WE'RE NOT TAKING THE MALE DEMONS WITH US?
IF THERE'S ROOM, BUT THE FEMALES FIRST, IN CASE THOSE BLASTED AIRSHIPS START BOMBING THE FOREST.
YOU HEARD THE COLONEL WANTS TO STERILIZE THE DEMONS?
WHAT A FOOL. WE NEED THEM TO BREED.
OUR SCIENTISTS ARE TRYING TO ENCOURAGE ADDITIONAL LILIUM DEVELOPMENT IN THE WOMB.
THIS IS HUMILIATING.
WE ARE MARIUM-BLESSED, CREATED TO BE HOLY WARRIORS -- AND WHAT DO THEY HAVE US DOING?
CHAINING DEMONS FOR TRANSPORT.
HOW IS IT OUR FAULT THAT WE WERE OUTNUMBERED IN RAVENNA, BETRAYED BY THOSE CURSED INQUISITRIXES --
Y-YOU... YOU'RE ONE OF US.
W-WHY ARE YOU H-HELPING THEM?
HOW *DARE* YOU?!
WE'RE *HUMAN!*
SMAK

OUT OF THE MOUTHS OF BABES.
CUMAEA WARP EVERYTHING, SOLDIER. REMEMBER THAT.
THE LAST TIME WE FOUGHT THIS WAR, THE LINES WERE CLEAR. BEAUTIFUL, EVEN. IT WAS HUMANS AGAINST DEMONS.

AND NOW WE'RE TURNING HUMANS *INTO* DEMONS.
I DON'T EVEN WANT TO KNOW WHAT'S NEXT.

WHEN DID THE RADIOS STOP RECEIVING?
THIRTY MINUTES AGO. WE THINK THE NEWLY ARRIVED DEMON SHIPS BEGAN JAMMING OUR SIGNALS.
COLONEL, JUST BEFORE THE RADIOS WENT OUT WE RECEIVED SOME...ODD PINGS... THAT WE CAN'T YET EXPLAIN. THE SIGNATURE WAS AERIAL, BUT LIKE NOTHING WE'VE EVER SEEN.

IT CAN'T BE OUR FORCES. OUR AERIAL REINFORCEMENTS ARE STILL A WEEK AWAY.
I WOULD URGE CAUTION, COLONEL. THE TROOPS WERE ALREADY UNNERVE BEFORE THE SIEG OF RAVENNA, AN THE ARRIVAL OF THE ENEMY'S AIRSHIPS HAS SHAKEN MORALE FURTHER.

SOME UNITS HAVE ALREADY ABANDONED THEIR POSTS. IF THEY FIND OUT THE DEMONS ARE GATHERING EVEN MORE FORCES --
THEY'LL STAND THEIR GROUND.
AND IF THEY DON'T, I WILL TURN THEM OVER TO THE CUMAEA FOR VIVISECTION. I'VE HEARD IT'S QUITE A HORRIBLE WAY TO DIE.
BE SURE TO TELL THEM *THAT.*

ER...YES, COLONEL.
SPEAKING OF THE CUMAEA...A MEMBER OF THEIR HIGH COUNC HAS ARRIVED. SHE HAS REQUESTED TO SEE YOU.
MAYBE WHEN I'M DEAD. WILL THAT BE SOON ENOUGH?
IT COULD BE. BUT WH TEMPT FATE?

COLONEL ANUWAT...SUCH A PLEASURE TO MEET YOU.
I AM THE LADY YVETTE LO LIM.
I'VE BEEN SENT BY THE CUMAEAN HIGH COUNCIL TO OFFER MY WISDOM DURING YOUR TIME OF NEED.

IF BY WISDOM YOU MEAN AIR SHIPS AND CANNONS, MAYBE I CAN SPARE YOU A MINUTE.
OTHERWISE, GOOD DAY.
OH, DON'T BE SALTY, COLONEL.
RAVENNA HASN'T GONE WELL FOR YOU, HAS IT? THERE HAVE BEEN A FEW BUMPS ALONG THE ROAD, YES? WAR NEVER GOES THE WAY WE WANT IT TO, MUCH LIKE LIFE.

WONDERFUL. A PHILOSOPHICAL WITCH.
I REMEMBER YOU NOW. FROM THE OLD DAYS.
YOU'VE BEEN IN SECLUSION FOR YEARS, HAVEN'T YOU? I HEARD RUMORS YOU BECAME UNSTABLE AFTER THE WAR.
DIDN'T GO WELL FOR YOU, EITHER, DID IT?

MAKES ME WONDER WHY THAT HIGH COUNCIL WOULD SEND YOU HERE, OF ALL PEOPLE. I THOUGHT THEY PRIDED THEMSELVES ON REASON.

LADY LO LIM! WHAT AN UNEXPECTED HONOR!
WHEN DID YOU ARRIVE? YOU MUST BE EXHAUSTED.
COME, LET US PREPARE A MEAL FOR YOU.

IN FACT, COLONEL ANUWAT...
...I DID COME BEARING GIFTS.
WHICH YOU'LL NEED VERY SOON IF YOU WANT YOUR TROOPS TO LIVE.

MY DAUGHTER IS THE ONE WHO HYPOTHESIZED YOUR KIND COULD BE CREATED WITH LILIUM... ENHANCED IN THE WOMB.
I'M PLEASED IT WORKED...

...THOUGH EVENTUALLY THEY'LL KILL YOU FOR NOT BEING HUMAN ENOUGH...

AH, BUT I SEE YOU ALREADY GUESSED THAT.

INDEED, YOUNG ZORTIA.
I COULD CERTAINLY USE HELP FROM SOMEONE WHO... UNDERSTANDS COMPLEXITY.

CONSTANTINE
"THE BARONESS, APPARENTLY, LEFT CONSTANTINE WITH A FLEET OF AIRSHIPS.
"IT SEEMS AS THOUGH HER NEGOTIATION DEADLINE WASN'T AS FIRM AS SHE LED US TO BELIEVE."

HER DEMANDS ARE RIDICULOUS, RESAK. MURDER ALL THE CUMAEA?
THE PRIME MINISTER WILL NEVER AGREE TO THAT.
I WOULDN'T BE SO SURE, ATENA.
THE CUMAEA ARE A MASSIVE THREAT TO HER HOLD OVER THE FEDERATION WITHOUT THEM SHE'D HAVE ACTUAL POWER INSTEAD OF BEING A GLORIFIED PUPPET.

YOU SUPPORT THIS, DON'T YOU?
I WOULD BE MURDERED. MY FRIENDS, PEOPLE I CARE ABOUT --

-- WHO COMMITTED ATROCITIES, REMEMBER?
NOT EVERY CUMAEA AGREES WITH WHAT'S BEEN DONE, BUT THEY'RE TOO FRIGHTENED TO CHALLENGE THE MOTHER SUPERIOR AND HIGH COUNCIL.
AND THE NOVICES... THEY'RE JUST CHILDREN. THEY ONLY KNOW WHAT THEY'VE BEEN TAUGHT.
ATENA, THE CUMAEA ARE A ROTTEN ORDER... AND THEIR NEED FOR LILIUM HAS BECOME UNCONTROLLABLE.
THEY WILL NEVER STOP HUNTING ARCANICS.
FATHER TAUGHT US TO DO THE RIGHT THING, NO MATTER THE PERSONAL COST.
SIGH
FATHER WARNED ME, BEFORE I AGREED TO SPY ON THE CUMAEA, THAT THE PRICE MIGHT BE TOO HIGH.
IF WHOLESALE MASSACRE IS THE ONLY WAY TO WIN, THEN HE WAS CORRECT.

ATENA... REMEMBER WHEN WE WERE CHILDREN...YOU'D COME HOME ON BREAK, AND FATHER WOULD TAKE US SAILING ALL THE WAY DOWN TO PONTUS?
IT WAS GOOD BEING IN A CITY WHERE HUMANS AND ARCANICS LIVED TOGETHER.
YOU'D CRY EVERY TIME WE HAD TO LEAVE --
OF COURSE I REMEMBER.
I WAS SO ANGRY TO BE A HUMAN BORN WITH POWER.
IT WAS UNFAIR THAT THE CUMAEA COULD TAKE ME FROM OUR HOME BECAUSE OF THAT.
BUT IT WAS THE LAW. IT STILL IS.
THAT'S WHY THIS ULTIMATUM IS SO WRONG. NONE OF THE CUMAEA HAD A CHOICE.
TELL THAT TO THE WITCHES WHO FLED THE FEDERATION. THEY CHOSE TO LEAVE RATHER THAN PARTICIPATE IN GENOCIDE.
THERE'S ALWAYS A CHOICE.
AHEM.
OH, DEAR. THIS IS QUITE THE ARGUMENT.
LADY ATENA AND COMMANDER RESAK, I PRESUME?
I AM NEKOMANCER REN MEMORIAN...AND I HAVE A PROPOSITION FOR YOU.

I SUPPOSE CORVIN BETRAYED MY IDENTITY.
OR THAT HATEFUL CAT.

NO ONE TOLD ME ANYTHING, TUYA.
I WAS ALWAYS HAPPY FOR YOU TO BE THE SMART ONE.
BUT THAT DIDN'T MEAN I WAS STUPID.

...SO...
THIS IS THE
MORTAL...WHO
HAUNTS YOUR
DREAMS...

...SUCH A HOLD...SHE HAS HAD... ON YOUR MIND...
...I THOUGHT... SHE MUST BE DEAD...
...I MISTOOK YOUR GRIEF...YOUR LOSS...
...I SEE NOW...WHAT YOU FELT...WAS BETRAYAL...
WHAT IS THAT THING SAYING, MAIKA?
MAIKA!
MISTER MONSTER IS SAYING YOU'RE A BAD PERSON.
AND THEY'RE GOING TO EAT YOU.

GO BACK TO SLEEP, ZINN.
...CHILD...
...THERE IS A TIME...TO SLEEP...
...A TIME TO HIDE...AND OBSERVE...
...AND A TIME...TO BE SEEN...AND FEARED...
...YOUR ENEMIES...MUST KNOW...YOU ARE NOT ALONE...
MISS... YOU NEED TO REMEMBER THAT, TOO.

WHAT... WHAT IS THIS?!
...I... KNEW...YOU WOULD COME...
...SO PREDICTABLE...
GODDESS.
GASP

YOU SMELL... LIKE AN OLD... ENEMY...
MAIKA! MAIKA, DAMN YOU, WAKE UP!
CONTRO THAT THING!
BITCH, *YOU* CONTROL IT.
ISN'T THAT WHAT YOU WANT?
GET BACK, FIEND! I WILL DESTROY YOU!
HOLD THAT THOUGHT.

FINALLY.
GODDESS, I USED TO BE BETTER AT THIS.
AH, MAIKA... THERE ARE YOU ARE.

GRANDMOTHER.
HOW *OVERJOYED* I AM THAT YOU FINALLY SUMMONED ME. MY HEART HAS NOT BEEN THIS WARM IN A THOUSAND YEARS.
IT'S PAINED ME BEYOND WORDS TO HAVE KEPT MY DISTANCE.
ALAS, I PROMISED YOUR MOTHER IT WOULD BE YOUR CHOICE.
AND LOOK HERE! SO MANY FAMILIAR FACES!
CLEARLY I INTERRUPTED A MOST FASCINATING REUNION.

WHAT A DELIGHT TO BE SURROUNDED BY FAMILY, IS IT NOT, GRAND-DAUGHTER?
YES. A DELIGHT.

An excerpt from a lecture by the esteemed **Professor Tam Tam,** former First Record-Keeper of the Is'hami Temple, and learned contemporary of Namron Black Claw...

CATS SETTLED THE KNOWN WORLD LONG BEFORE THE ARRIVAL OF THE ANCIENTS. IT WAS, BY ALL ACCOUNTS, A TIME OF PEACE -- THANKS TO OUR UNIFICATION UNDER THE WISE BANNER OF ADARA FARCLAW.
THE SCHOLARSHIP OF THE POETS WAS IN ITS INFANCY, SO PERHAPS THAT IS WHY THERE ARE NO TRUSTED RECORDS DESCRIBING THE MOMENT WHEN ANCIENTS DISCOVERED THIS WORLD, OR HOW THEY FIRST APPEARED TO OUR ANCESTORS.
THERE ARE LEGENDS, OF COURSE. THAT THE ANCIENTS HAD NOT YET ADOPTED THE FORMS WE SEE THEM IN NOW. THAT THEY WERE, IN FACT, MADE OF LIGHT INSTEAD OF FLESH -- AND THAT THEY DID NOT SETTLE THIS WORLD IMMEDIATELY, BUT DEPARTED AND DID NOT RETURN FOR FIVE HUNDRED YEARS.
WHY? SOME SAY IT WAS UBASTI HERSELF WHO DROVE THEM AWAY THE FIRST TIME.

IT IS SOMEWHAT STRIKING THAT WHEN THE ANCIENTS DID RETURN, IT WAS A SMALL GROUP, SMALLER THAN WHAT FOLLOWED LATER, AND THAT SOME OF THEIR QUEENS WORE THE FORMS OF THE JAGARAN.
IT IS ALSO SIGNIFICANT THAT THESE ANCIENTS DID NOT SETTLE THE LANDS TO THE NORTH, UNLIKE THOSE WHO ARRIVED LATER -- AND WHO FORMED THE DUSK AND DAWN COURTS.
INSTEAD THEY VENTURED DEEP INTO THE SOUTHERN SEAS TO CREATE A UNION WITH THE WAVE EMPRESS, WHO IS THE SECOND OF UBASTI'S GREAT ALLIES.
THE WAVE COURT ESTABLISHED ITSELF ON AN ISLAND FEW HAVE VISITED, AND WHOSE NAME IS PROTECTED BY THE SIRENS. THEIR ANCIENT SECRETS ARE AS MUCH A MYSTERY AS THE DEEP, AND THEIR ARCANIC CHILDREN WHO VENTURE INTO THE WORLD SEEM AS IGNORANT OF THE WAVE COURT'S FULL POWER AS THE REST OF US.
ODD, THAT THE DUSK AND DAWN COURTS BARELY ACKNOWLEDGE THE WAVE COURT'S EXISTENCE. THE POETS WOULD TELL YOU IT IS BECAUSE SOME BITTER ENMITY REMAINS UNRESOLVED BETWEEN THEM.
BUT OTHERS... SUCH AS MYSELF... SPECULATE THERE IS A MORE DISTURBING REASON.
THAT THE ANCIENTS OF THE DUSK AND DAWN ARE AFRAID OF THE WAVE COURT...AND DO NOT WANT TO DRAW ITS ATTENTION.

CHAPTER THIRTY-THREE

BITCH.

ZINN SLEEPS?
IF YOU CALL IT THAT.
I DO NOT KNOW HOW YOU HAVE ACCUSTOMED YOURSELF TO SUCH A PARASITE.

FORTUNATELY, I AM HERE NOW.
YOU WON'T HAVE ANYTHING MORE TO FEAR FROM YOUR AUNT, I PROMISE YOU THAT. AND IN THE DAWN COURT, YOU'LL BE EVEN SAFER.
YOU'LL SO ENJOY ITS PLEASURES. A GRANDDAUGHTER OF THE WOLF, MAKING HER TRIUMPHANT RETURN! WHAT A JOY THAT WILL BE.

JUST THINK, NEVER AGAIN WILL YOU NEED TO SET FOOT IN SOME IMPOVERSHED FRONTIER TOWN. THIS PLACE REEKS OF BLOOD AND EXCREMENT.
WAR IS ALWAYS SO... DISENCHANTING.
HMMM.

THAT DISAPPROVING SOUND...
...YOUR MOTHER MADE NOISES LIKE THAT.

YOU EVEN LOOK LIKE MORIKO.
I FIND THAT... STARTLING.
WHY? THE WARLORD IS HER TWIN. YOU SEE HER FACE ALL THE TIME.
IT'S NOT THE SAME. THEY WERE TWO VERY DIFFERENT WOMEN.

BUT YOU...HAVE MORIKO'S ASPECT IN YOUR FACE. HER INTENSITY...HER NARROWING EYE.
I FIND MYSELF NOSTALGIC FOR MY DAUGHTER WHEN I SEE YOU.

YOU SHOULD HAVE SUMMONED ME WHEN SHE DIED. I WOULD AVE SAVED YOU. YOU WOULD HAVE BEEN SPARED...A GREAT DEAL.
I LOST THE NECKLACE BEFORE THE WAR. WHEN I FOUND IT AGAIN...IT WAS TOO LATE. THE HARM HAD BEEN DONE.
AH.

NONETHELESS... I AM HEARTENED THAT MORIKO SHARED MY PROMISE TO PROTECT YOU.
LIKE YOU PROTECTED THE SHAMAN-EMPRESS AND HER CHILD?

THE CHILD LIVED. IN THE END, SHE WAS PROTECTED.

ACCORDING TO THE BLOOD FOX, THE COST OF THAT PROTECTION WAS CAPTIVITY AND EXPERIMENTATION.
AND YET, HERE YOU ARE, INHERITOR OF THE BLOOD. SHE...AND THE SHAMAN-EMPRESS...MIGHT ARGUE THAT IT WAS WORTH THE SACRIFICE SO THAT YOU MIGHT EXIST.

FOR WHAT PURPOSE, GRANDMOTHER?
THE DUSK COURT... OR WHOEVER THE BARONESS REPRESENTS...WANTS MY POWER FOR THEMSELVES.
MY AUNT WANTS THE SAME THING.
FORGIVE ME IF I ASSUME YOU'RE NO DIFFERENT.

HA.
DO YOU KNOW WHAT YOU ARE?

AN OBJECT OF ENVY. A CREATURE THAT DEFIES OUR BOUNDARIES...A REPRESENTATION OF POSSIBILITIES THAT ARE TERRIFYING WHEN WE EXAMINE THEM TOO CLOSELY.
I SHOULD KILL YOU. PART OF ME THOUGHT OF DOING SO, LONG AGO.
BUT PERHAPS I'VE... SOFTENED.
IRONICALLY, YOU ARE PART OF ME...AND THE PRODUCT OF A BRILLIANT, DANGEROUS MIND.
YOUR MOTHER'S MIND.
AND SO I ALLOW MYSELF TO BE CURIOUS ABOUT THE FULLNESS OF YOUR POTENTIAL.

EVERYONE THINKS MY POTENTIAL IS LIMITED TO MURDER.
MY MOTHER THOUGHT THE SAME.

DID SHE?
THAT WOULD BE A DISSERVICE TO YOUR MOTHER'S IMAGINATION.

NOW... SUMMON ZINN, IF YOU WILL.
THE OLD GOD AND I NEED SOME TIME ALONE.

"LADY LO LIM...WHEN YOU SAID YOU HAD A WEAPON THAT WOULD SAVE MY TROOPS, I EXPECTED THAT WE'D BE ABLE TO USE IT *BEFORE* THE DEMONS BEGAN FIRING ON US.
"INSTEAD, THE FOREST IS BURNING, AND SO ARE MY SOLDIERS."
"COLONEL ANUWAT...A DEVICE OF THIS COMPLEXITY HAS TO BE ASSEMBLED WITH CARE...UNLESS YOU WISH FOR IT TO EXPLODE IN YOUR FACE."
RADIO SIGNALS ARE STILL JAMMED. WE HAVE NO WAY OF KNOWING WHEN THOSE OTHER DEMON SHIPS WE DETECTED WILL ARRIVE.
TELL THE OFFICERS TO CONTINUE REMOVING OUR TROOPS TOWARD THE BORDER WALL.
SURELY YOU'RE NOT PLANNING A RETREAT, COLONEL?
WHAT HAPPENED TO YOUR RUMORED VOW TO NEVER SURRENDER?
THERE ARE NO ABSOLUTES IN BATTLE. WHEN A SITUATION CHANGES, THE WISE CHANGE, TOO.
AND THAT CANNON IS A BIT SMALL FOR THE DISPLAY OF POWER YOU'RE STILL PROMISING ME.
SMALL, BUT DEADLY. MUCH LIKE YOU, YES?
YOU DON'T REMEMBER...BUT WE'VE MET BEFORE.
AT SETHIHAR, DURING A FUNDRAISING GALA FOR THE ACADEMY. IT WAS ONLY IN PASSING.

OF COURSE I DON'T RECALL THOSE DAYS. THE WAR DESTROYED FRIVOLITY.
BUT IT DIDN'T DESTROY EVERYTHING, DID IT?
WHAT IS ON YOUR MIND, COLONEL ANUWAT?
A MEMORY.
YOU SPENT THAT WHOLE EVENING WITH MORIKO HALFWOLF, WHO HAD COME TO FETCH HER DAUGHTER FROM THE ACADEMY.
I'M SURE YOU'RE MISTAKEN. I DON'T KNOW ANYONE BY THAT NAME.
PAH.
YOU'RE HERE BECAUSE MAIKA HALFWOLF IS IN RAVENNA.
THAT'S THE REASON I'M PULLING BACK MY TROOPS.
YOU DON'T GIVE A FUCK WHETHER WE LIVE OR DIE. SHE'S YOUR MISSION. THE ONLY THING I'M *NOT* CERTAIN OF IS *WHY.*
HEH... HEH HEH...
SHE'S MORE THAN A MISSION, COLONEL. SHE'S MY *LIFE.*
ARE YOU READY TO DESTROY ARCANIC AIRSHIPS, COLONEL?

THE PAST.
"I ADMIT...I WAS NOT EXPECTING TO MEET YOU AGAIN LIKE THIS."
...BELOVED... DO NOT LEAVE US...
...WE NEED YOU...
ABOMINATIONS!
WE CANNOT LET THE CHILD LIVE.
"NOR AM I FOOLISH ENOUGH TO THINK WE CAN FORGET...OUR CONFLICTS."
SHE WILL DESTROY EVERYTHING.

THE PRESENT.
BUT I DO HOPE WE CAN PUT ASIDE HARD FEELINGS.
I'D LIKE TO THINK WE'VE BOTH CHANGED OVER THE YEARS.
THAT EXPERIENCE HAS GRANTED US...A HIGHER WISDOM.

WELL.
PERHAPS YOU'LL AT LEAST AGREE WE SHOULD NOT DRAG MAIKA INTO OUR PAST?

...WHICH PAST...
...THE ONE WHERE YOUR KIND...WERE STARVING AND BROKEN... LITTLE MORE... THAN WRECKED SCAVENGERS...
...THE PAST... WHERE YOU POSSESSED BODIES...NOT YOUR OWN...
...THE PAST... WHERE YOU ENSLAVED... MORTALS...AND TRANSPORTED THEM TO THIS WORLD --

-- *ENOUGH,* ZINN.
YOUR HYPOCRISY IS TEDIOUS. YOU, THE GREAT MURDERER... YOU AND YOUR SISTER-BROTHERS, LOST IN EXILE, DEVOURING EVERYTHING IN YOUR VILE PATH --

-- OH. HELLO, DEAR.

I THINK YOU TWO HAVE BEEN ALONE LONG ENOUGH.

TSK, GRANDDAUGHTER.
WHERE IS YOUR AUNT?
BLOWING UP THE FOREST OUTSIDE RAVENNA. FOR SOME REASON, SHE SEEMS... IRRITATED.
OH, YOU

AND THE BARONESS? HAVE YOU HAD YOUR OWN... RECONCILIATION?

RECONCILE WHAT?
THE BARONESS IS A STRANGER TO ME.

HMMM.
PACK YOUR THINGS, GRANDDAUGHTER. WE'LL BE DEPARTING SOON.

I FELT YOU VIBRATING FROM THE OTHER SIDE OF THE TOWER.
I'M SURPRISED RAVENNA DIDN'T EXPLODE FROM THE TWO OF YOU BEING IN A ROOM TOGETHER.
...SHOULD I NOT...BE FURIOUS...?
...SHOULD I NOT...DESIRE VENGEANCE...?

...THE ANCIENTS IMPRISONED... MY KIND...
...THEN DID WORSE...TO THE BELOVED...

I KNOW. I CAUGHT A GLIMPSE, REMEMBER?

BUT ZINN... I SHARE HER BLOOD.
I NEED TO KNOW HOW YOU FEEL ABOUT THAT.
...YOU FEAR...I MIGHT PUNISH...?
MAYBE.

...CHILD...

...I AM NO... FOOL...

...I CANNOT AFFORD... REVENGE...
...I LACK FULL STRENGTH...AND YOUR MORTALITY...IS MY WEAKNESS...SHE COULD EASILY... KILL YOU...
...IF YOU DIE... I SLEEP...AND THAT CANNOT BE...
...NOT BEFORE...I REMEMBER...
YOU ALSO DON'T WANT TO RETURN TO MY FATHER.
...THAT WOULD BE... EXHAUSTING...

...YOU SHOULD HAVE WARNED... YOU WERE SUMMONING... THE WOLF...
...YOU CANNOT... TRUST HER...
MY MOTHER SAID THE SAME THING.

SHE ALSO SAID THAT WHEN BARGAINING WITH FAMILY...
...TRUST ONLY GETS IN THE WAY.

SIGH
GAK!
HSSSSS
I DID WARN YOU.
NNGH!
GET... OFF...
AAAAAHH!
THAT WILL DO.
SMASHH
PANT PANT
WHY, CORVIN?
WHY WOULD YOU THROW AWAY YOUR LIFE...WHY WOULD YOU THROW AWAY THE HONOR OF YOUR FAMILY...FOR MAIKA HALFWOLF?

HAVE YOU ASKED *YOURSELF* THAT QUESTION, BARONESS?
YOU COULD HAVE KILLED THE HALFWOLF YEARS AGO, WHEN SHE WAS AT HER MOST VULNERABLE... HARVESTED HER BODY FOR THE DUSK COURT.
YOU, WHO WERE AT CONSTANTINE. YOU, WHO WITNESSED FIRSTHAND HOW HER BLOOD AWAKENED.
BUT YOU DIDN'T TELL A SOUL WHAT SHE DID. YOU PROTECTED HER, PRETENDED SHE WASN'T THE ONE.
THE QUESTION IS...WHY AREN'T YOU PROTECTING HER NOW?
SHE WON'T LIVE, CORVIN...NO MATTER WHAT WE DO. YOU KNOW WHAT THE ORACLES SAID.
THE BLOOD SERVES ONLY ONE MISTRESS, AND IT ISN'T HER.
IT'S A GOOD THING, THEN...THAT I PUT MY FAITH IN THE GODDESS AND NOT ORACLES.
...HEH.
YOU REALLY *HAVE* CHANGED... BROTHER.

MISS, IF YOU AND THE BARONESS WERE FRIENDS, WHY IS SHE TRYING TO HURT YOU?

WELL... YOU'VE BEEN ANGRY WITH ME BEFORE.

NOT LIKE THAT.

LITTLE FOX, REMEMBER WHO I WAS WHEN WE FIRST MET.

WHO I STILL AM.

YOU'RE THE FORGIVING TYPE...BUT NOT EVERYTHING CAN BE FORGIVEN.

TAKE THAT LETTER TO CORVIN.

TAY WITH HIM. ON'T FUCKING EAVE HIS SIDE NTIL I COME TO YOU.

IF YOU MAKE ME GO SEARCHING, YOU'LL BE WEARING YOUR *TAIL* AROUND YOUR *NECK.*

I ALMOST BELIEVE THAT, MISS.

BYE, MISTER MONSTER!

ENJOY YOUR BOOK!

...WHAT...A PECULIAR... CHILD...

...IF I EAT... THIS ONE... WOULD THE WOLF...MISS HER...?
...IT WOULD BE... SATISFYING...TO KILL...ONE OF HER CHILDREN...
WHY IS THAT MONSTROSITY GROWLING, WHELP?
IS IT ABOUT TO ATTACK AGAIN? AND WHY IS IT GROWING OUT OF YOUR BODY?
WELL?
WHAT HAPPENED TO THE DOGS?
WHAT ARE YOU TALKING ABOUT?

MY MOTHER NEVER SPOKE OF HER CHILDHOOD... UNLESS IT WAS ABOUT YOU.
IT WAS A WAY OF KEEPING YOU CLOSE, I SUPPOSE.

SHE TOLD ME THAT WHEN YOU WERE SMALL, A CUMAEAN ENVOY ARRIVED, AND THERE WERE PUPPIES ON THE SHIP, FRESH BORN.
THE HUMAN SAILORS DIDN'T WANT THEM, DUMPED THEM IN THE WATERS OF THE PORT.
YOU HATED THAT.

SO YOU SET THEIR SHIP ON FIRE.

MORIKO... TOLD YOU THAT STORY?

THE PUPPIES DROWNED, OF COURSE.

ARCANICS DON'T KEEP DOGS.

YOU'RE THE WARLORD, AUNTIE. AND MORIKO IS DEAD.
YOU DON'T NEED TO KEEP REPEATING THE LIES YOU BOTH TOLD YOUR MOTHER.

HOW *DARE* YOU BE SO FAMILIAR WITH ME.
WE MIGHT BE RELATED BY BLOOD, BUT YOU'RE NO NIECE OF MINE. YOUR MOTHER ABANDONED THIS FAMILY.

I DON'T CARE WHAT THAT THING IS... OR HOW MUCH PROTECTION YOU'VE BEEN GRANTED BY THE WOLF QUEEN AND MY... THE BARONESS.
YOU ***WILL*** GIVE UP MORIKO'S SECRETS. YOU ***WILL*** TELL ME WHAT YOU KNOW OF THE WEAPON THAT DESTROYED CONSTANTINE.
AND IF YOU DENY ME, I WILL OBLITERATE YOU.

TO QUOTE A FRIEND OF MINE...
... "THAT FALSE BRAVADO MUST GET VERY TIRING."

TRUST ME, I KNOW. MY MOTHER ONCE COMPARED ME TO YOU, AND IT WAS NOT A COMPLIMENT.
THOUGH, IT WAS ALSO ONE OF THE QUALITIES MY MOTHER LOVED ABOUT YOU... IN MODERATION.
THAT IF YOU DIDN'T LIKE SOMETHING, YOU'D TRY TO CHANGE IT.

EVEN IF IT DIDN'T GO WELL FOR YOU.
ENOUGH. YOU WON'T... YOU CAN'T... DISTRACT ME --

MY MOTHER'S DEAD. YOUR SISTER'S DEAD.
AND WHAT I AM MAY BE A MYSTERY, BUT IT'S NOT MUCH OF A SECRET.

THAT IS AN OLD GOD. WE SHARE THE SAME BODY. IT'S A BLOOD INHERITANCE, AUNTIE.

AS MUCH AS YOU AND I ARE WOLVES, I'M SOMETHING ELSE, TOO.

YOU THINK I KNOW WHAT DESTROYED CONSTANTINE. AND I DO.

IT WAS ME, AUNTIE. *I* DESTROYED CONSTANTINE. ME AND THE OLD GOD, TOGETHER.

WE WERE HUNGRY.

BOOM!
BOMBS!
IMPOSSIBLE!
MY AIRSHIPS PUSHED THE FEDERATION FROM RAVENNA'S WALLS!
GODDESS.
NOT FAR ENOUGH, IT SEEMS.
KRAKADOOOOM
OUR SHIPS ARE GOING UP LIKE PAPER.
TANNO...IT'S THE SAME WEAPON THAT DROVE US FROM THE LILIUM REFINERY.
CURSE THOSE WITCHES.

WZZZZHHH
MASKS SECURE?
YES, MA'AM!
THEN AIM HIGH! WE NEED TO SEND THESE CANNISTERS OVER THE WALL!
BOOM!
BOOM!
RUN!
DON'T BREATHE THE AIR!
G-GODDESS --
KOFF KOFF
KOFF KOFF
KOFF
GRRR!
RRAWWRRRR!
RRRRRR!

OH, DEAR.
OUR FLEET... UP IN FLAMES.
WHAT A TERRIBLE, UNEXPECTED... SHAME.
SNIFF SNIFF
THAT SMELL...
NNGH!

"MISTER CORVIN, IT'S JUST LIKE THE MADNESS IN PONTUS. BUT HOW?"
ARRRGH!
AIIEE!
HOLD THE DOOR AGAINST THEM!
CHOOM
CHOOM
CHOOM
CHOOM
QUESTIONS LATER, KIPPA. DON'T KNOW HOW MUCH TIME WE HAVE LEFT."
YOU'RE CERTAIN THE TUNNELS ARE CLEAR?
THE GREY RIDERS HAVE BEEN STANDING GUARD SINCE THE HALFWOLF ORDERED THEM REOPENED. NO FEDERATION TROOPS ARE NEARBY.
IT'S A NARROW WINDOW, BUT THE HUMANS MIGHT STILL BE DISTRACTED WITH THEIR ATTACK ON THE FLEET.
YOU AND I ARE LEAVING RAVENNA.
NOT WITHOUT MISS!
YES, WITHOUT HER. I GAVE MY WORD.
THE LADY HALFWOLF HAS BEEN SECRETLY ORGANIZING THIS EVACUATION FOR DAYS, IN CASE THE FEDERATION LAUNCHED ANOTHER ATTACK.
THE KIND OF ATTACK WE CAN'T DEFEND AGAINST --
BOOM!

WHAT MADNESS IS THIS?!
THE SAME FUCKING INSANITY THAT TOOK PONTUS.
SOMEONE WEAPONIZED IT.
SURELY NOT EVERYONE CAN BE AFFECTED?! WHERE ARE THE CIVILIAN TROOPS?
OCCUPIED WITH OTHER BUSINESS, IF WE'RE LUCKY.
LUCKY?! WE'RE TRAPPED HERE, WHELP! WE NEED THEM TO DEFEND THE CITY AND THE WOLF QUEEN!
...TASTE...FOUL... TAINTED...BY THE ESSENCE...OF A SISTER-BROTHER...
...I CANNOT EAT...TOO MANY...
...I MIGHT BE POISONED...AS I WAS...ON THE ISLE OF BONES...
ZINN...THE BLOOD FOX USED YOUR KIND AS A DRUG TO ENHANCE HIS POWERS --
WHERE'S THE WOLF --
RRYAAHH!

MONSTER!
LOOKS LIKE YOU'RE GETTING THAT FIGHT, AFTER ALL.

A moment with **Professor Tam Tam,** former First Record-Keeper of the Is'hami Temple, and learned contemporary of Namron Black Claw...
"...FROM THE DARKNESS WE EMERGED, RESURRECTED INSIDE NEW SELVES WE COULD NOT HAVE DREAMED OF BECOMING...
...AND OUR ENEMIES, WHO THOUGHT US DEAD, WHO TRIED TO MURDER US WITH HATE, FLED FROM OUR REBIRTH, IN DESPAIR AT HAVING MADE US STRONGER..."

AN EXCERPT FROM THE JOURNALS OF ADARA FARCLAW, LITTLE ONES. I READ IT EVERY YEAR, AS A REMINDER OF WHAT RESILIENCE AND HOPE CAN GIVE US -- IF ONLY WE ARE PATIENT.

WINTER, AFTER ALL, DOES NOT LAST FOREVER. NOR DOES HARDSHIP, OR INJUSTICE.

THIS IS A TIME FOR RENEWAL...

...SPRING HAS ARRIVED.

CHAPTER THIRTY-FOUR

RAWWRR!!
...FINALLY... THIS...IS THE FACE...I REMEMBER...
...YOUR HATE... IS THE TRUEST... THING ABOUT... YOU...
MOTHER!
STOP!

FFFT!
=GASP=
I'M YOUR DAUGHTER!
YOU DARE INTERFERE?!
BOOM!
TRAITOR!
WHAT -- NNGH -- HAS HAPPENED TO HER?!
I TOLD YOU, IT'S THAT POISON!

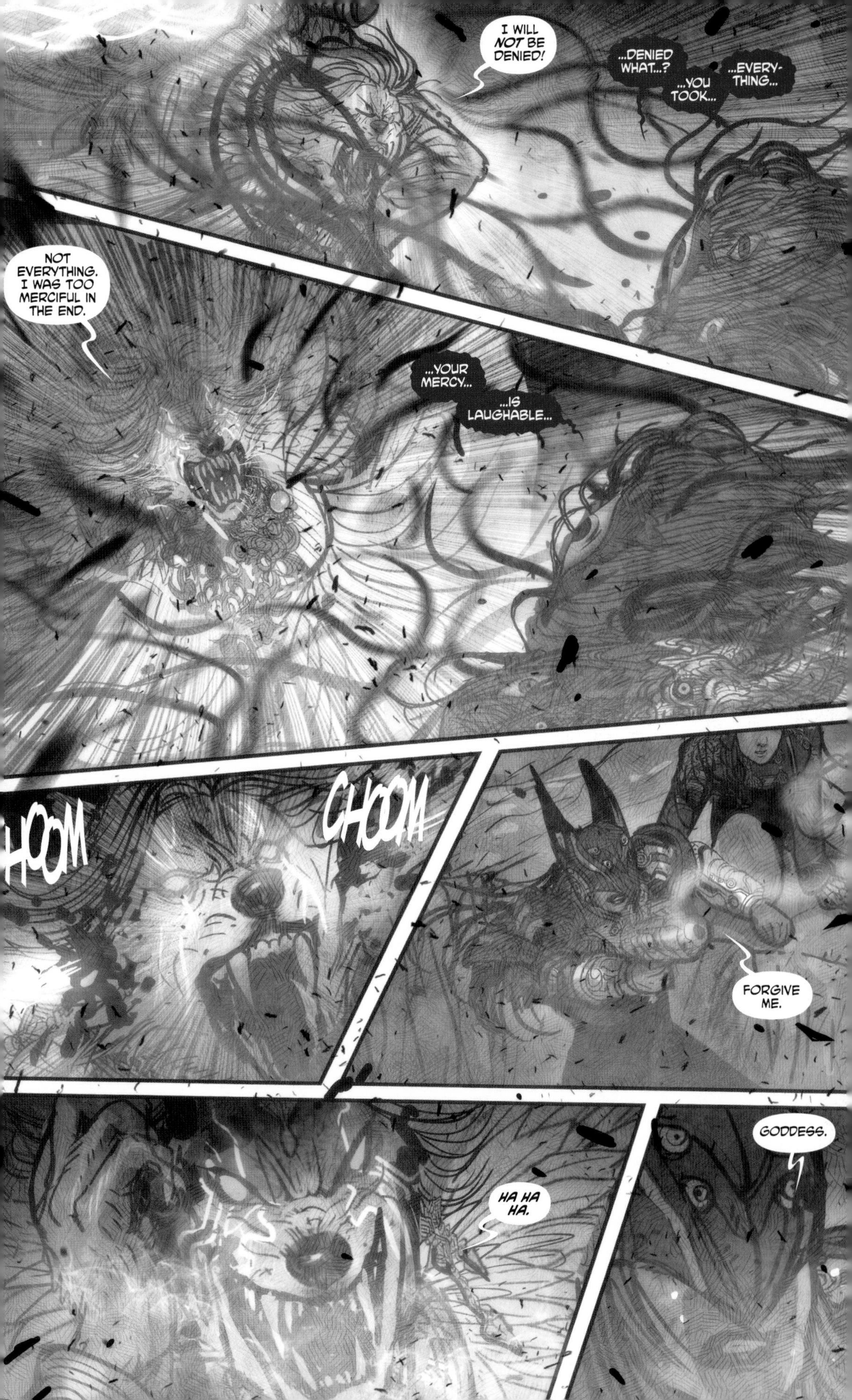
I WILL NOT BE DENIED!
...DENIED WHAT...?
...YOU TOOK...
...EVERY-THING...
NOT EVERYTHING. I WAS TOO MERCIFUL IN THE END.
...YOUR MERCY...
...IS LAUGHABLE...
HOOM
CHOOM
FORGIVE ME.
HA HA HA.
GODDESS.

HOW SUCH A WEAKLING SPRANG FROM MY WOMB, I WILL NEVER KNOW.
...ENOUGH... WITH YOUR RANTING...
...THE VANITY... OF YOUR SPECIES...
...ARE YOU... NEVER SATISFIED...?
RWAAR!
ARE YOU SATISFIED, ZINN?

GAAAH! THERE'S TOO MANY!
FUCK! HOLD ON!
CHKK
SHOMP
CHOOM
I DON'T DESIRE YOUR HELP!
CHOOM
I DON'T CARE. ARCANICS NEED YOU.
I NEED YOU.
I CAN'T LET YOU DIE JUST YET.

HIISSS!
...CHILD...
...WE CANNOT ALLOW...
...OUR HEARTS...
...TO BREAK US...
YOU'RE RIGHT, ZINN.

HALFWOLF, RUN!
RRAAWWRRRR!!
GODDESS...
HALFWOLF, HURRY, MY SHIELD WON'T HOLD!
HEH.
...STOP...
...NOT THE MASKS... REMEMBER THE LAST TIME...
...WE CANNOT HOLD...THE POWER...
WE HAVE TO TRY.

ZINN... THE MASKS ARE SILENT. I DON'T FEEL ANYTHING, EITHER. MAYBE THIS TIME WILL BE DIFF --

HOLD US
RELEASE US
DREAM US
DESIRE US
BEGIN US

SING US
BECOME US
FIGHT US
LOVE US
US
BEAR US

OLD GODS, I SILENCE YOU.
YOU CANNOT HAVE THEM.
THEIR PURPOSE IS NOT YET REVEALED.
...BELOVED...
THE UNION NOT YET COMPLETE.
...BELOVED...

...BELOVED...
SHUT UP AND FIGHT, ZINN.
CORVIN! MISS!
I'M COMING!

RAAAAAH

I SO ENJOY WHEN YOU SURPRISE ME.
YOU CREATE SO MANY... OPPORTUNITIES.

ONE DAY, PERHAPS, YOU'LL APPRECIATE *MY* SURPRISES JUST AS THOROUGHLY.

CLICK

THE HALFWOLF... SHE'S USING THE MASK... THE FRAGMENTS... ARE AWAKE...
...THE SONG... THE SONG... TELL ME WHOSE VOICE... YOU HEAR...

YIP YIP
THE INQUISITRIX! THE MOTHER SUPERIOR! WHAT'S WRONG WITH THEM?
TSK. THEY'LL SHAKE IT OFF.

BUT THIS IS A *FASCINATING* TURN.
I CAN ONLY IMAGINE WHAT HAS AWAKENED INSIDE THIS BOX.

...THE GREAT MASK...
...CURSE THE SHAMAN-EMPRESS...
...THAT IS OUR BIRTH-RIGHT...
I'LL TEAR IT FROM YOU.
STAY BACK! LET THEM FIGHT!
WAKE UP, MOTHER!
REMEMBER YOURSELF!
I DO.

AND WHAT...
...GRANDMOTHER...
SVVASHHH
ARRGH!
...WILL I TEAR FROM YOU?
NNGH!
MISS!
YOU HAVE TO STOP!
CHOMP
RAWRR!
SHRRIIIPP

...TASTES SO GOOD... YOUR BLOOD... GLOWS...EVERY DROP... BURNING...
GAH! I HEAL FASTER THAN YOUR TEETH!
...BURNING...
MAIKA!
...WHO... WHO ARE YOU...
MISS!

MISS! LISTEN TO ME!
IF YOU DON'T STOP, YOU'RE GOING TO KILL US ALL!
YOU'LL TEAR OPEN THE SKY!
...KIP...PA...?
GRAAHHHRR!!
...KIP...PA...?
"FUCK."

I THOUGHT THE MASKS WOULD GIVE US MORE POWER.
...THEY DID... WE ARE NOT DEAD...
...BUT ITS POWER... IS TAINTED...
...A MIRACLE... WE HAVE NOT... BEEN OVER-WHELMED...
...YOU GLIMPSED... WHAT WAS... WAITING... FOR US...
...THE SHAMAN-EMPRESS MASTERED THIS MASK BEFORE, DIDN'T SHE?
...YES... BUT SHE WAS... THE BELOVED...

...THIS GAMBLE... IS WEAKENING... THE PRISON... OF MY KIND...
...AND WILL DESTROY... OTHER LIVES...
...WITHOUT EVEN... THE BENEFIT... OF FEEDING...

YES, WE MIGHT LOSE. IF IT'S NOT A LACK OF POWER, THEN IT'S BECAUSE WE'RE DISORGANIZED.

...DISORGANIZED...?
...SHE WILL DEFEAT US... BECAUSE WE ARE NOT... *WHOLE*...
...IT IS WHY... MY KIND... LOST... OUR WAR AGAINST THEM...

...WE... WERE DIVIDED...
...WE DID NOT TRUST...

...IT WAS... MY FAULT THEN... AND MY FAULT NOW...
...I HAVE NOT... BEEN GENTLE... I HAVE NOT... BEEN LOYAL...

I DON'T KNOW ANYTHING ABOUT YOUR WAR WITH THE ANCIENTS... BUT WITH ME, WHY WOULD YOU BE GENTLE? WHY WOULD I?
I BLAMED YOU FOR WHO I AM. AND YOU BLAMED ME FOR BEING A PRISONER.

BUT YOU DIDN'T MAKE ME.
JUST LIKE I WASN'T THE ONE WHO TIED YOU TO MY BLOOD.

...I SPEAK OF TRUST...
...BUT I FEAR TRUST...
...I FEAR... HOW I WILL CHANGE...

FUCK, ZINN.
CAN IT BE ANY WORSE THAN WHO WE ARE NOW?

BESIDES, SOME THINGS WON'T CHANGE.
LIKE HOW I WOULD GIVE MY LIFE FOR THAT GIRL.
THE SAME WAY I'D GIVE MY LIFE FOR YOU.

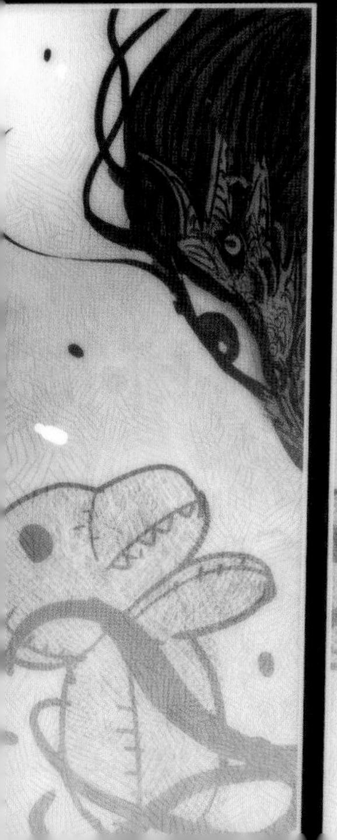

...THEN LET US SAVE...THE CHILD...

...WITH THAT ONE ACT...WE BEGIN...

NO.

KOFF
KOFF
KIPPA.

YAY!
AND YOU DIDN'T KILL US!
YOU'LL NEVER STOP RUNNING TOWARD DANGER, WILL YOU?
YOU NEEDED ME, MISS.
WHAT HAVE YOU BECOME?
I DON'T KNOW YET.
GASP
I... I --
AIIEE!

TUYA, ARE YOU HURT?!
N-NO. I DON'T THINK SO.

YOU'RE SAFE. DON'T BE AFRAID...
IT'S JUST ME.
MAIKA --
NO. DON'T TELL ME WHY.

CHAPTER THIRTY-FIVE

We made a vow, Tuya...
Do you remember?
It was right after the war.
WE MUST FLEE!
UBASTI CURSE YOU! THESE ARE THE ONLY COPIES LEFT OF THE JAGUA CODEX! WE HAVE TO SAVE THEM!
That who we were before - how we were raised, what we were taught - none of that should matter.
Surviving had remade us.
It was a chance to be new.
I never told you why
I wanted that so badly.
And you never told me.
HURRY! I HEARD THERE'S STILL SHIPS OUTSIDE RAVENNA!
You called it..."The beautiful dream."
Too bad we gave up on dreams.
THIS IS MADNESS!

WE'LL NEVER BE ABLE TO TAKE OFF WITH ALL THESE PEOPLE! THEY'LL TEAR THESE VESSELS APART!
YOU HAVE TO STOP THEM FROM BOARDING!
A LITTLE LATE FOR THAT.
THIS SHIP IS DESIGNED TO CARRY TROOPS IT CAN HANDLE THE --
GODDESS, SAVE US.
MIN... MAKE SPACE FOR THE WOLF QUEEN.
AND SEE TO THE WARLORD. SHE'S BEEN INJURED.

DON'T... GO... FAR...
TRY AND CATCH ME, AUNTIE.

...NO...NOT CATCH...
...NEED HELP...NEED... YOU...
...NOW... RIGHT NOW...
WIFE, CALM YOURSELF.
I THINK SHE'S PRETTY FUCKING CALM.

I'M NOT ABANDONING YOU.
BUT YOU'LL PROBABLY REGRET HAVING ME AROUND.

ISN'T THAT RIGHT, BARONESS?
COME, LET'S TAKE THIS ELSEWHERE. NO ONE WILL BOARD WITH US STANDING HERE.

GOOD.
THEY *SHOULD* BE WARY.

HMMM.
I LOVE CHAOS, DON'T YOU?
IT MAKES IT SO EASY TO SLIP INTO PLACES UNNOTICED.
HELLO, YVETTE.
SUCH A STRIKING CHANGE IN APPEARANCE, MAIKA.
THE MASKS, YES? YOU USED THEM TO TRANSFORM YOURSELF? I CAN HEAR THEM... SINGING.
IF YOU WOULD ONLY LET ME TOUCH THEM --
SHUT UP.
I SUSPECTED YOU'D BE NEARBY.
MY FATHER IS THE ONLY ONE WHO COULD HAVE WEAPONIZED THE BLOOD AND FLESH OF AN OLD GOD.
WHO ELSE WOULD HE SEND TO CONVINCE THE FEDERATION TO USE IT?
I HEAR THE EFFECT IS QUITE... DRAMATIC.
IT'S FUCKING AWFUL.
HE STARTED THIS WAR WHEN HE BOMBED AURUM...AND NOW HE'S HELPING KILL ARCANICS.
YOU WISH TO KNOW WHY?
YOU SAID IT YOURSELF. CHAOS MAKES IT EASY TO SLIP INTO PLACES UNNOTICED. HE'S BREAKING THE WORLD, SO THAT HE CAN TAKE POWER.
OF COURSE. BUT IT'S FOR YOUR BENEFIT, AS WELL.
TO CONTROL ME?
AND PROTECT YOU.

YOU ARE A WALKING IRONY, MAIKA HALFWOLF.
PERHAPS THE MOST DANGEROUS CREATURE IN THIS WORLD. AND YET, THE MOST VULNERABLE.
YOUR ENEMIES ARE ENDLESS.
YOU'RE ONE OF THEM.
AM I?

IS *HE?*

SOMEONE -- FIND LADY LO LIM. I WANT TO KNOW WHAT WAS IN THOSE CANNISTERS WE SHOT INTO RAVENNA.
SOMETHING UNNATURAL HAPPENED IN THAT CITY.
ER... LADY LO LIM IS GONE. SHE WAS LAST SEEN RUNNING TOWARD RAVENNA, ACCOMPANIED BY --
COLONEL, WE FINALLY HAVE VISUALS ON THE AIRSHIPS!
AND?!
THEY'RE NOT OURS! BUT THEY DON'T LOOK LIKE DEMON SHIPS, EITHER! WE'VE NEVER SEEN THIS DESIGN BEFORE!
POWER THE CANNON! PREPARE TO FIRE!
WAIT... SOMETHING IS WRONG --
BOOM!

WE'RE UNDER ATTACK! TAKE COVER!
SISTER ZORTIA! WHERE ARE YOU?!
AAIIIEEEE!!

DID YOU SEE THEM BOMBARD THE FOREST?!
THEY MUST HAVE KILLED ALL THE HUMANS!
BURN THEM! BURN THEM!
HAHAHA. YES, BURN THE HUMANS. BURN THEM ALL.
BY THE GRACE OF THE BLOOD AND THE LIGHT!
PERMISSION TO BOARD! WE HAVE FOOD AND MEDICAL SUPPLIES!

ARE THOSE PEOPLE ALL THAT'S LEFT OF RAVENNA, SENTENUS? DID SO MANY TRULY DIE?
WE COULD HAVE COME SOONER.
AGREED. THE PLAN WOULDN'T HAVE BEEN AFFECTED.
YES, IT WOULD HAVE.
RID YOURSELVES OF REGRET, WAR-MASTERS. OTHERWISE WE'LL NEVER PREVAIL.

SO, YOU'RE THE SAVIORS NOW?!
WHAT A FUCKING JOKE!
YOU'RE THE JOKE, HALFWOLF! YOU AND YOUR INCOMPETENT AUNT!
YOU SHOULD BE GUTTED! ALL THAT POWER, AND RAVENNA WAS LOST UNDER YOUR WATCH, NOT OURS!
THE BLOOD IS WASTED ON YOU!
TELL ME SOMETHING I DON'T KNOW!
WE FIGHT WITH THE WEAPONS WE HAVE!
AND SOMETIMES NEITHER WE NOR OUR WEAPONS ARE GOOD ENOUGH!
BUT IF YOU GET LUCKY, YOU GET ANOTHER CHANCE TO FIGHT.
AND I'M A LUCKY WOLF.
THE BLOOD IS LIFE.
THE BLOOD IS LIGHT.

I HOPE THE SAME IS TRUE FOR YOU, WAR-MASTERS.
IF YOU'VE BENT THE KNEE TO THE OLD MAN... YOU'RE GOING TO NEED EVERY SCRAP OF LUCK YOU CAN GET. HE THINKS OF YOU ALL AS SLAVES TO HIS PLANS... NOT AS PEOPLE.
WE'RE NOT SLAVES, HALFWOLF... WE'RE LOYAL.
LET ME KNOW THE DAY YOU DISOBEY HIM.
AND THEN I'LL CALL YOU FREE.
CHILD... BEWARE... HER BLOOD...
...A FAMILAR SCENT...
I KNOW THE OTHER WAR-MASTERS... BUT NOT YOU.
I AM THE *BEAST.*
AND I WILL SEE YOU IN THE NORTH, HALFWOLF. WE HAVE AN APPOINTMENT WITH THE DUSK COURT... TO DISCUSS WHO WILL LEAD THE WAR EFFORT.
GOOD.
WE'LL BE ABLE TO COMPARE GIFTS FROM THE OLD MAN.
WHAT A REFRESHING YOUNG KILLER.
I REALLY DO NEED TO CONVINCE HER TO BE MY SWORD-NOVICE.
DAMN HER!
KRRRAK!

AURUM.
YOU MUST REST, MOST HOLY MOTHER! WHATEVER HAPPENED CLEARLY WEAKENED YOU!
WE CANNOT AFFORD TO HAVE YOU ILL. NOT NOW! YOU ARE THE HEART OF THE FEDERATION --
GET AWAY FROM ME...
...OR I WILL EAT YOUR SOUL.
SHE'LL EAT MORE THAN THAT.
THIS IS INTOLERABLE. WHY DOES IT PAIN US SO WHEN THE HALFWOLF USES THOSE MASKS?
SURELY YOU HAVE SOME INSIGHT, HAVING WORN THEM YOURSELF?
I'VE SHARED MY INSIGHTS, REMEMBER? NO ONE CARED.
STOP ACTING LIKE A HURT FOOL.
THIS IS IMPORTANT. WE DIDN'T KNOW WHEN YOU USED THEM. WE HAD NO IDEA UNTIL YOU RETURNED AND TOLD US.
WHY IS IT DIFFERENT FOR --
BOOM!

AH, IF IT'S NOT MY OLD TEST SUBJECT.
IT'S THE FATHER!
FEED! FEED NOW! WE NEED STRENGTH!
URK!
CALM YOURSELF --
HOW EASY IT IS TO EXPOSE YOUR KIND.
GASP
YOU WEAR YOUR POWER SO POORLY.

LOOK UPON THEM! YOU ARE LED BY DEMONS!
SWEET MARIUM!
BLAM!
BLAM!
BLAM!
OUR MOTHER SUPERIOR HAS BEEN POSSESSED!
AIIEEE!
SHHLUKK!
I SHOULD THANK YOU.
THE BLOOD I COLLECTED FROM YOU MADE ALL THIS POSSIBLE.

CHOOM!
I APPLAUD YOUR EFFORTS TO FEED OFF ME.
BUT DESPITE ALL APPEARANCES, YOU AND I SHARE ONE THING IN COMMON.
WE ARE *GODS.*
I JUST HAPPEN TO BE THE SUPERIOR ONE.

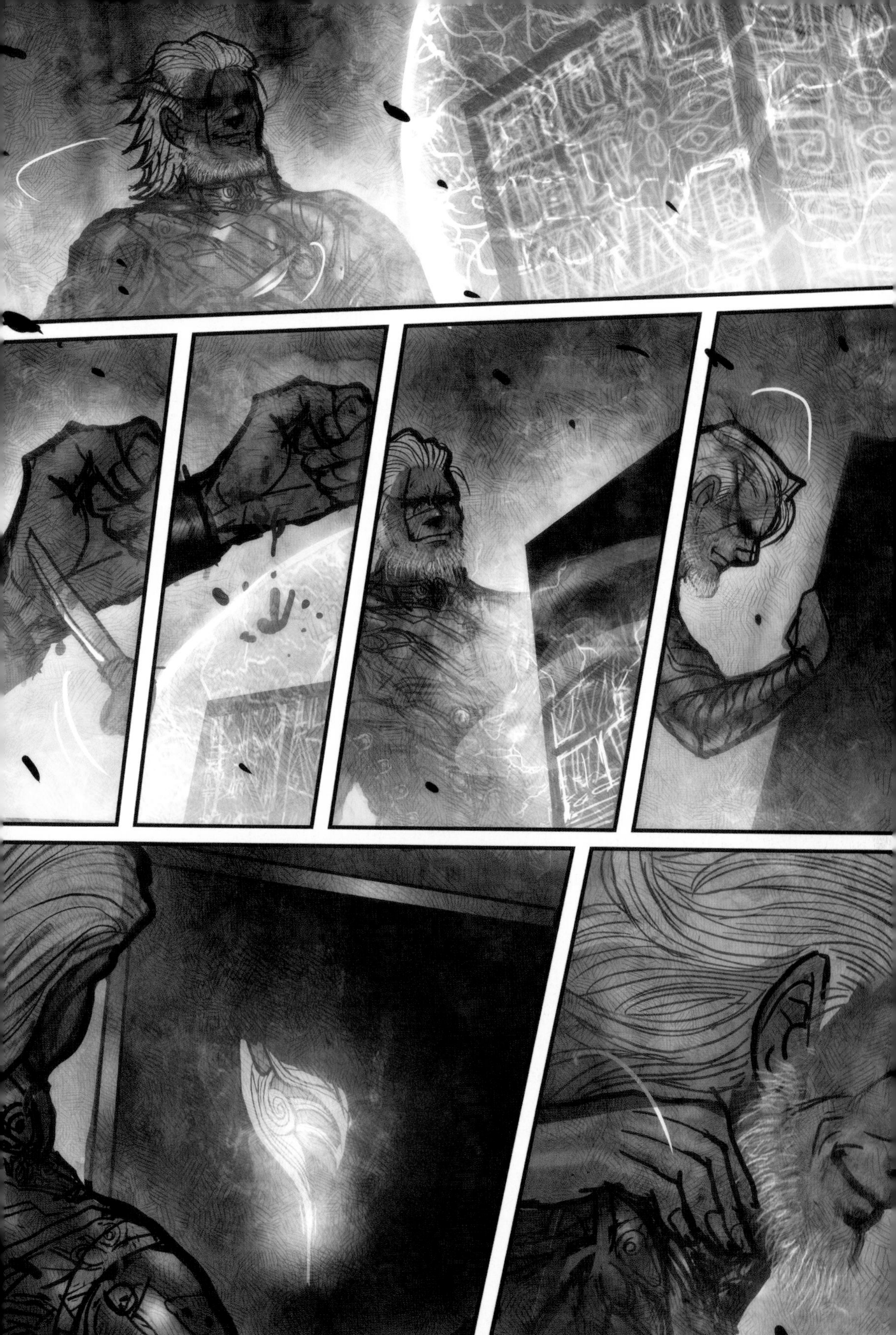

TSK, TSK. SO MUCH VIOLENCE.
AND FOR WHAT? SOMETHING THAT WE BOTH KNOW DOESN'T *REALLY* BELONG TO YOU?
HUMAN.
YOU HAVE AN ABUNDANCE OF ARROGANCE.
INDEED, LORD DOCTOR. AS DO YOU.
WHO ARE YOU?
AN OLD ACQUAINTANCE.
KRAK
NNGH!
VIHN.
HOW DID I NOT SEE YOU THROUGH YOUR ILLUSION?
I KNEW WE WOULD MEET AGAIN. HERE, IN FACT. YOU WOULDN'T HAVE SENT ANYONE ELSE TO FETCH THIS MASK FRAGMENT.
AND SO I MADE SOME... ADJUSTMENTS TO MYSELF.

THE DIFFERENCE BETWEEN YOU AND ME, LORD DOCTOR, IS THAT YOU BELIEVE THAT YOU ARE BRILLIANT.
I, HOWEVER, PREPARE AS IF I AM NOT.
SVASH!
KRASH!
THAD
YOU'VE ENHANCED YOUR STRENGTH AS WELL, VIHN.
THE CORPSE OF THE OLD GOD THAT FELL IN PONTUS? YOU MADE A SERUM FROM ITS BONES?
THE BLOOD FOX CAN'T BE THE ONLY ONE TO BENEFIT FROM HIS DISCOVERIES.

YOU CANNOT USE THE MASK. BUT I CAN. MY DAUGHTER CAN.
I AM DOING THIS FOR US ALL. THE ANCIENTS, THE OLD GODS, ALL THE CREATURES WHO FLED TO THIS WORLD FOR REFUGE.
DO YOU NOT WISH TO RETURN TO THE STARS?
NNGH!
YOU FOOL! THOSE ROADS ARE GONE...FOR A REASON. THE SAME REASON THE SHAMAN-EMPRESS HAD TO DIE.
SHE WAS TOO CURIOUS, AND DID NOT RESPECT THE DANGERS OF WHAT WE ESCAPED FROM.
NEITHER DO YOU. YOU CANNOT RECKON THOSE HORRORS.
BUT I CAN. I HAVE SEEN ZINN'S MEMORIES.
AND I AM NOT AFRAID.
THIS IS WHY YOU CANNOT BE ALLOWED TO REASSEMBLE THE MASK.
IN THIS, I THINK THE OLD GODS AND THE ANCIENTS WOULD AGREE.
DO WE ALL WANT THE MASK? OF COURSE. BUT ONLY SO THAT WE MIGHT LIVE MORE COMFORTABLY ON *THIS* WORLD.
INDEED. YOU BOTH PREFER YOUR PRISONS TO A LIFE OF FREEDOM.
YES, WE CHOOSE A SOFT DEATH OVER A HARD LIFE.
HAPPILY.

THIS IS NOT THE DAY YOU PLANNED FOR, LORD DOCTOR.
YES, YOU SURPRISED ME. I SUPPOSE ONE DAY I WILL THANK YOU FOR THAT.
NO, YOU WON'T.
I TOLD YOU.

GODDESS, THAT FEELS STRANGE.
LIKE I'M LOSING PART OF MYSELF.

...EVEN I...FEEL COLD...
...BUT EVEN...MORE PECULIAR...
...I AM NOT...AS HUNGRY...

WAS IT LIKE THIS WITH YOU AND THE SHAMAN-EMPRESS? WHEN SHE WORE THE MASK?
...WE DID NOT...TAKE... THIS FORM...
...WE DID NOT... MERGE...
...WE COULD NOT...

...BUT I THINK...YOU ARE...PART OF ME...AND I AM...YOU...
...AND THAT...IS THE DIFFERENCE...
WE'VE NEVER SPOKEN ABOUT THAT, HAVE WE? NOT DIRECTLY.
YOU HAD A CHILD WITH THE SHAMAN-EMPRESS. SOMEHOW...SHE MADE THAT POSSIBLE.

...THE CHILD... YES...
...SHE WAS...SHE WAS... MINE...
THAT CHILD IS MY ANCESTOR.
AND YOU ARE MY...
...MY...
FAMILY, MISS.
MISTER ZINN IS FAMILY.
LIFE IS VERY STRANGE, ISN'T IT?
...STRANGER... THAN I... COULD HAVE DREAMED...

GO LOOK AFTER CORVIN. THAT IDIOT CAN BARELY STAND.
WHERE ARE YOU GOING?
TO CHECK ON THE WOLF QUEEN.

BE CAREFUL, MISS.

AS SOON AS YOU START LISTENING.

NEVER.
NEVER.

I THOUGHT WE'D KILLED HER, FOR SURE.
...HER KIND...ARE DIFFICULT...TO EXTERMINATE...
WHILE SHE... REGENERATES... SHE WILL BE... AS IF DEAD...

ZINN... WHEN WE KILLED THE BLOOD FOX ON THE ISLE OF BONES... I ONLY STRANGLED HIM.
...INDEED...
DID HE SURVIVE THAT?
...UNDOUBTEDLY...

BUT THE FERRYMAN, REN... THEY ALL SAID HE WAS DEAD. EVEN VIHN.
...THE TRICKSTER LIED... AND THE FERRYMAN AND REN... WOULD NOT KNOW... BETTER...

YOU DIDN'T SAY ANYTHING!
...YOU DID NOT... ASK...
...I AM NOT... RESPONSIBLE... FOR CORRECTING... YOUR LACK OF... EDUCATION...

FUCK. ARE ALL THE ANCIENTS AS POWERFUL AS THE WOLF QUEEN?
...YES...
...THEY ARE... FORMIDABLE FOES...
THEY COULD CRUSH THE HUMANS, ZINN. THE WOLF QUEEN, BY HERSELF, COULD WIN THIS WAR.

THEN WHO WOULD THEY RULE? WHO WOULD AMUSE THEM?

Not so long ago, I was still wishing I'd never left you.

Another life, Tuya. Another dream.
PRIVACY.
...AS YOU WISH...

You and I were told so many lies.
Lies about who we had to become, and who we had to fear.
...BUT HAVE CAUTION...

How different things would have been if we'd stopped listening.
If we'd focused instead on what we had right in front of us...each other?

But I know how impossible that would have been.
More impossible than anything that's happened since.
YOU COULD HAVE JUST SAID YOU WANTED TO KILL ME. ALL THOSE YEARS AGO.
I WOULDN'T HAVE MINDED. I MIGHT HAVE HELPED YOU.

Who I am now... could not have been born any other way... except through leaving you.
BUT YOU WAITED TOO LONG. NOW I WANT TO LIVE.
I HAVE... THINGS TO DO.
I was rotting inside, Tuya.

was a rot.
poison.
YOU'VE CHANGED.
YOU'VE CHANGED SO MUCH YOU'RE NEW TO ME.
And now I'm something else.
MAKES YOU UNCOMFORTABLE, DOESN'T IT?
IT WAS EASIER TO BETRAY ME WHEN I WAS CRUEL. EASIER TO BETRAY ME WHEN YOU REMEMBERED MY CRUELTY.
I don't know what that is yet, Tuya.
'm not good.
NO, IT DIDN'T MAKE IT EASIER.
YOUR CRUELTY WAS JUST PAIN. I KNEW THAT. BUT IT MADE ME ANGRY.
WHY COULDN'T YOU JUST FUCKING HEAL, MAIKA? WHY COULDN'T YOU SWALLOW YOUR PAIN LIKE THE REST OF US HAD TO?
IF YOU'D JUST CONTROLLED YOURSELF --
ut maybe...just
aybe...I might be
ood for something.
IF I PRETENDED, YOU MEAN.
PRETENDED TO BE HAPPY. PRETENDED TO BE SAFE.
PRETENDED NOT TO BE FURIOUS AND TERRIFIED AND CONFUSED.
ne day I hope
o understand
hat that is.
IS THAT WHAT IT WOULD HAVE TAKEN, TUYA? TO KEEP YOU FROM KILLING ME?
BECAUSE PRETENDING WOULD HAVE KILLED ME ANYWAY.
Will you be there when I do?

≠SNORT≠
WHAT?
REALLY, TUYA? YOU HAD TO FUCK MY AUNT?
SHUT UP.
FFFT!

TUYA.
SHHUK!
...BETRAYAL!...
GYAHH!
I COULDN'T BE SURE CORVIN HADN'T WARNED YOU ABOUT THE SERUM AND HOW IT WAS ADMINISTERED.
SO I HAD SOMETHING DIFFERENT CRAFTED. JUST AS EFFECTIVE.
TU...YA...
IT'S JUST YOUR MIND, MAIKA.
IT'S LIKE GOING TO SLEEP.
YOU WON'T FEEL ANYTHING WE DO TO YOU.
IF IT MAKES IT EASIER, I WON'T HARM THE FOX CHILD.

TO BE CONTINUED...